I0829403

CRYPTO BIZARRO

A COMPENDIUM of OBSCURE HORRORS

Limbs
by
Josh Leichliter

I flex to impress
I lift out of need
One is for hunger
the other for greed

Sometimes I jump
Though often I fall
Bound by these floors,
Ceilings and walls

With these I can grasp
I can stab or betray
I can feel, I can hug
Or caress you all day

I can kick, I can stomp
I can blacken your face
I could hike, or climb
Countless vistas await

One quick impulsive
decision to make,
Am I a monster
Or am I okay?

Illustrated by Josh Leichliter
Edited by David J. Lovato

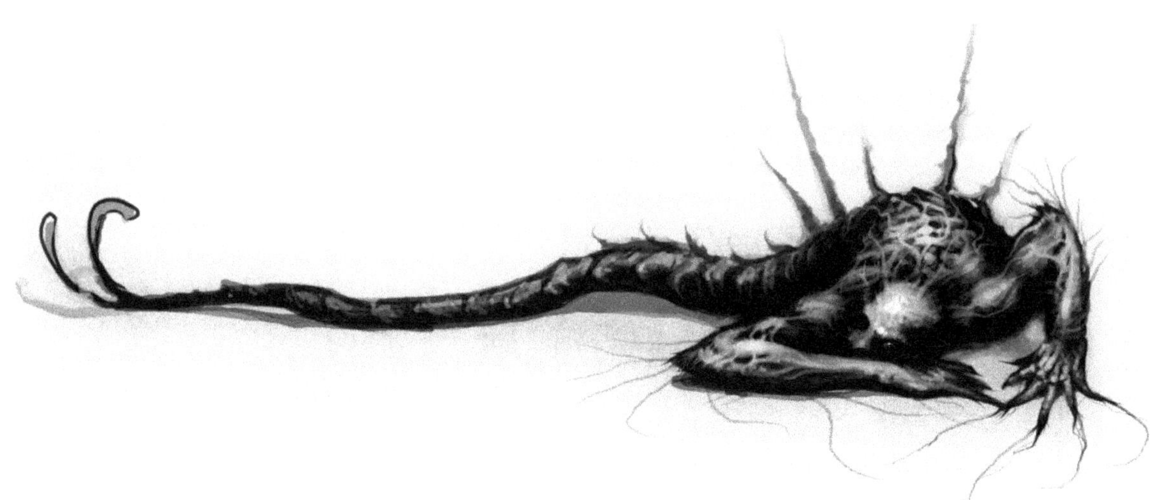

Table of Contents

Devoured by Love
by
Josh Leichliter

They walked hand-in-hand down an endless stretch of road. They couldn't remember their names, or where they were going. But they remembered that they loved each other.

He gazed at his companion. She was beautiful. Shiny black curls framed her petite face, her complexion was pale as snow. Her lips curled in an affectionate smile as the dim summer sunlight accented her perfect features. She stared back at him from holes where her eyes used to be, blood curdled around the sockets like smeared mascara. To him, she was the most stunning thing ever conceived. Simply beautiful.

He loved her. And she loved him. They had started the day as any other, awakening happily in each other's arms. But this day was different; there was to be some ceremony, something special. They ate a nice breakfast and went for a walk in the park, when... something happened. Everything changed.

They remembered none of that now, only that they loved each other. Together they stumbled down a ruined road, hand-in-hand. They clambered along like a couple of broken marionettes, disintegrating a little more with every step. By now their organs were exposed and dragging along the ground, painting a wet trail of their affection behind them.

Grabbing a handful of her hair, he bit violently into her face and tore a large chunk of her flesh away. With each mouthful she became more beautiful, and his love grew more intense. As did hers. Stabbing her hand into his open torso, she wrenched free a coiled piece of intestine and attacked it hungrily. They devoured each other as they shambled in loving embrace, sharing their hearts in the most tangible way.

It Sits on the Stairs
by
David J. Lovato

"Well, our time's just about up," I said.

"Thank you, again," Jackson replied. He wiped at the corners of his eyes; he hadn't fully cried in weeks, but he had teared up. "Can we schedule the next appointment?"

"Actually, I don't think that'll be necessary." Jackson looked confused. "I think we've made plenty of progress, and in my opinion, you don't need to come in anymore."

A smile cracked on his face. "You sure?"

"If you disagree, let me know. But I think you're ready to take on the world, Jackson."

He stood up, crossed the small space between my couch and his, and shook my hand.

"Thank you so much, Dr. Rubins."

"It's not all me," I said. "You've done great work these past few months."

I tried to remind all my patients of that, but it was truer for Jackson than anyone I'd ever treated. He'd come so far from his stay in the psychiatric ward. When I first met him, he was confined to a small room, where he spent *Z ulb lbq ulb lx ylxh lx z kvdeq, wdh hor urlgru lejltx udbx ylxhru.* most of his waking life carving a message into every surface he could:

It sits on the stairs.

"Dr. Rubins," Jackson said. The smile left his face, the vigor drained from his handshake. "What if... What if I see it again?"

"You won't. It's not real, Jackson. It never was. And you've moved past it." Jackson let go of my hand. He stared into nothing, which worried me. "You know you can call me at any time, for any reason. I'm here for you, Jackson. So are your friends and family."

Normality returned to his face, his posture. "You're right. I can do this. Thanks again, Dr. Rubins."

"Good luck, Jackson."

Jackson Yates was easily my most famous client, and one of my toughest. But he was one of my strongest, and as the months went by, I thought of him less and less. I had other patients who needed my attention. When he called me just after 5 A.M. one morning, I answered the phone without even paying attention to who was calling.

"Dr. Rubins," I said.

A man was sobbing on the other end of the line. I sat up, more awake, and looked at the contact info. Yates... yes, I remembered.

"Doctor... It's back. I see it."

"Jackson, where are you?"

"I'm at home. It never moves, I told you that." He sobbed, every word came out strained, like he had to drag it from his throat. "It just sits there. On the landing. Oh God, I can see it right now."

"Jackson, have you stopped taking your meds?"

"No."

I didn't believe him. How could I?

"Jackson, listen to me. There's nothing on your landing. Nothing there. Whatever you think you're seeing—"

"It was faded at first. Like a trick of light. But once you see it, you don't un-see it, Doctor. That's how it was the first time. Then it started back up again." He broke into tears. "I tried not to, I tried..."

"Jackson. There's nothing on your stairs. Maybe you think you see something, but there's nothing there. Tell you what, take a picture, and send it to me."

I thought back to his sketches, his descriptions: long fingers, empty eye sockets, the whole thing pale white like a skeleton, but smoky, wisps and tendrils flowing off of it. ...Did something creak in my house? Of course not.

"I have the picture."

"Can you see it?"

"Yes," Jackson said. "Even in the picture. I see it."

"Send it to me."

A few seconds later, my phone vibrated. I was apprehensive, but if Jackson could be this strong, surely I could. I opened the picture.

"...It's an empty staircase. That thing doesn't exist, Jackson."

"What do I do?"

"Jackson, let's try what we talked about. Do you remember when we talked about what you could do if you ever saw it again?"

He paused, and even his sobbing diminished. "Yes. Walk past it."

"Just go upstairs. Pay it no attention. You'll realize it's all in your head. Do you think you can do that for me, Jackson?"

"Yeah, Doc. I think I can."

"I can come over, if you need."

"No, no. I have to get through this. I can't let what happened before happen again. I won't."

"You sure, Jackson?"

"Yes, Doctor Rubins."

"I'll stay on the line, okay? Just take this one step at a time."

"One step..." I heard shuffling, like he had been sitting on the floor by the wall, and now slid up it for support. "Okay. First step."

"You got this, Jackson."

He took a step, sniffed hard, waited... and took another. Then another.

"You're doing great," I said.

"It's looking right at me."

"No it isn't. It isn't real."

Another step, and another. Then I noticed something.

"Jackson, how charged is your phone?"

"It's full."

"Do you ever lose reception at home?"

"No, I'm in a good spot. Why are you asking?"

"...Just making sure the call won't drop," I said. It was only partially a lie. I could hear faint static, but it was nothing. It would pass, surely.

Another step, and another, and the static grew louder.

"I'm on the first stair."

"You're doing fine, Jackson. Can you take another step?"

I heard the wood groan beneath his foot. He waited for a long time, and then I heard another step—barely. The static was so loud. But he was doing wonderfully, I couldn't distract him now.

"Oh my God, Doctor Rubins. Oh God."

"Jackson, what's wrong?"

"It's right in front of me. Just one step up, on the landing. I can see it so clearly."

I could barely make out his words through the static.

"Jackson. It isn't real."

"...I know, Doctor. But it *looks* real."

"I know it does. But you can't let it control you."

"Yeah." He took another step, then started crying. "It's on the landing with me."

"Then take another step, Jackson. Keep going. Leave it behind you."

"...Yeah. You're right, Doc."

Seconds passed, so slowly. Then, through the white noise pouring out of my phone's speaker, I heard another soft footstep. Then another.

I grinned widely. "You did it, Jackson."

"Doctor Rubins, I—"

The soft static turned into a high screech, like microphone feedback. I ripped the phone from my ear; it was so loud I could still hear it. Then it went dead as the call dropped.

I dialed Jackson's number, but the phone went straight to voicemail. I left him a message, then tried again. Nothing. I stood up off of my bed and grabbed my coat from where it hung on the closet door.

Jackson's front door was locked when I arrived. When he didn't answer it, I called the police. I gave them Jackson's information; considering his past, it wasn't hard to get them to take me seriously. They brought in a battering ram and knocked in the front door, and even from behind the patrol car, I could see Jackson's body at the bottom of the stairs.

When they cleared the scene, they invited me in to identify him. It was so hard to see Jackson like that; lying at the bottom of the stairs, his head twisted completely around, his left leg snapped, a jagged piece of bone sticking up into the air, still dripping blood, tattered pajamas clinging to it.

The human mind is so fragile. I imagine he went downstairs to get a drink of water, just like anyone might on any given night, and then this thing his mind conjured up came back to haunt him. He must've slipped and fallen. Jackson Yates, once my greatest success story, almost even a friend, and now this.

The next few nights, I lay awake thinking over our sessions. The things he said, the way he talked... I had no doubt that this creature was real to him. But there was something off about it, something different from most of my patients who suffered from delusions. Jackson seemed somehow more... true.

I told the police I'd left some notes in his bedroom. Since the scene was no longer active, the police chief, an old buddy of mine, didn't mind giving me the house key. As silly as it was, I decided I wouldn't go near the place at night, so the next afternoon, I drove over to Jackson's house and unlocked the front door.

The stairs were just beyond it. The blood had been cleaned, so there was a shiny spot just at the base of the stairs, but the steps higher up were dusty, worn-looking. And the landing...

It was empty. Of course. I thought long and hard about the things he'd said. Jackson was convinced he wasn't crazy, that he had tapped into something or some place humans aren't meant to see, and once you do, your world overlaps with it, it stretches thin and things poke through.

Before I knew it, an hour had passed. Now and then I thought I saw something, maybe a tendril of smoke, maybe a finger... but it was always a trick of the light, or just a shadow blending in with the little corner table resting on the landing. Now I was only thinking of what I was doing here. I turned to leave—

And stopped. Did I just...? No, of course not. I stared at the landing some more. Still empty. When did it get so dark in here?

My eyes crossed a little. Jackson explained one time that it was like one of those picture puzzles, where you cross your eyes to see an image, and it might take a while, but you'll eventually see it, and then it gets easier every time.

But why would I *want* to see this?

Maybe because part of me believed Jackson was telling the truth. Maybe part of me needed to know that he wasn't delusional, that there are things we don't understand, things not touched on in any of those hundreds of books on the shelf in my office.

"Okay," I said to myself. "I'll walk in his shoes."

One step, then another. I was on the bottom stair. I forced myself to lift my leg, move it forward, put it on the next step. Up I went, until I got to the step before the landing. One last look, I scanned for anything. But I was alone; I'd never been so alone. Up I went.

Onto the landing. Then the next step; somewhere around here was where Jackson tripped. Up another step. I closed my eyes, held my breath, half expected some ethereal hand to reach out of that other place, grab my ankle, and rip my feet out from under me, just like it did to Jackson.

But that was crazy. And nothing happened. I went up another step.

Up and up I went, feeling more confident with every step. At the top I could see the door that led to the upstairs bedroom, where Jackson once slept, where he knew peace for a few short months before his tragedy. And that's all it was, a simple tragedy. I stopped outside his door. My eyes began to water. Poor Jackson.

I turned around, and screamed when I saw it sitting on the stairs below me, waiting for me to come back down.

The Headsman and the Corpse
by
Josh Leichliter

They look at me.
When I lop them off and they roll into the basket.
Sometimes they land face up,
sometimes they stare at me.

I stare back.
I look into their eyes, wondering what they're thinking.
If they're thinking.
I think they are.

I once got a smile.
She just smiled and stared.
Didn't blink.
Just smiled.

I smiled back.
It was only polite.
I wonder if she went to Heaven.
Maybe she was innocent, after all.

That's not my job.
I can't think about that.
My job is to chop.
Just to chop.
Chop, chop, chop!

Since I was fourteen I've chopped.
Chopped them all.
Peasants, criminals, merchants and kings.
Doesn't matter.
They all chop the same.
Come right off,
if you do it right.

Pa was a headsman too.
I chopped him when I was sixteen.
I'm old now and the day is here.
It's only tradition.

Danny-boy is sixteen today.
I've taught him as Pa taught me.
He's very talented!
I'm excited to see him,
from the basket.

I told him to turn me 'round,
if I land face down.
Turn me 'round Danny-boy! Haha!
Such a good son.
I want to see him and smile.
Let him know how proud I am.

I hope I can still smile.
I'm gonna try real hard.

It's time.
Time to get chopped.
My turn in the basket.
I'm sad to go, but...
It's only tradition.

Here we go.
Be strong, Danny-boy.
I know you sharpened that axe,
just like I taught ya.

WHUMP!

Wow.
Didn't feel a thing.
Good job, son. Ya did real good!
Nice and clean, just like I taught ya.
I'm proud of you.

Turn me 'round now boy.
Better hurry!

There we go, that's right.
Hi Danny!
I smile.

Danny has tears in his eyes.
Just like me, when I chopped Pa.
Dumb boy. I love you, son.
I...

Qj bcppv, jv wcni. Ray qy
zijdezb d bdupqtqui, dez vca
dwldvb bdqz vca'z zc
devykqem tcp ji.

Won't Forget
By
David J. Lovato

"Never forget where we come from, Grub," Bother said.

Grub held a tiny pinkish shoe out before him, waiting for Bother to take it, but Bother only stared.

"The bad place?" Grub said. It was all so long ago, Grub was so young then.

"Yes. No." Bother took the shoe, looked it over, and then disappeared into a hole at the base of a tree, the one that led to their collection. He returned a few minutes later, the shoe gone.

"Grub don't understand," Grub said. Bother pressed his bulbous head against Grub's.

"The big people, *they* don't understand. They hate us, Grub. That's why we take. They did this to us, the things in the bad place. Made us. Made us to hate us, Grub. So we take what they love."

Nana spoke up; Grub thought she had been asleep. "We take enough of what they love, maybe they love us?"

"They can't love," Grub said. "Can't love nothing but their things. Their shinies."

Bother ran his fingers through Grub's patchy hair, then put a hand on his own head. Bother had no hair; his gigantic, lumpy head was adorned only with a large scar, running from behind one ear, over the top, to behind the other. "They took," Bother said. "So we take. Maybe they don't forget what they did. Maybe they don't do it again. That's where we come from."

Grub clicked his teeth together, trying to think. A few flashes of the bad place came back, the big people in their awful white clothes, their bad shinies, the ones that cut and took and stitched back together.

"You understand now, Grub?"

Grub grunted. "Grub's head don't work."

Nana got up from the shade of the tree and hugged him, so softly.

"Bother won't be around forever," Nana said. "None of us will."

Grub's eye twitched. "Not long left to make them understand, then?"

"Suppose not," Bother said. "Beside the point. Trying to say goodbye, Grub."

"Goodbye?" Grub's heart beat faster, pressure built up around his eyes. It made his head feel larger; he knew it wasn't, but it felt like it. He wrapped his arms around his head as if to hide it in shame.

"Grub come back from taking one day, and Bother won't be here anymore."

"Don't!" Grub shouted. Bother raised his hands to quiet him.

"Been around too long already, Grub. Too much pain. Head hurts most. Don't be sad for Bother."

Grub wiped at his eyes with the palms of his hands. "Fine. Relief for Bother. Sad for Grub."

Bother too hugged Grub, and the three of them, the last of their kind, stood in embrace for a moment. "Fine," Bother said. "Sad for Grub. But not forever."

"Not forever," Grub said. "But won't forget."

Bother passed in his sleep a few days later. Grub cried endlessly; sometimes quietly, sometimes loud, shrieking noises. Nana tried to quiet him, to tell him if any big people came through their neck of the woods, they'd hear, come find them, maybe kill them, but Grub didn't care. Sad for Grub.

He tried to remember that Bother was relieved now, that all of the things that happened in the bad place were gone now, and Bother even looked restful as Grub and Nana found some of their sharper shinies and dug a little hole in the earth beneath Bother's favorite tree. They put his limp, stocky body in the dirt, then covered it back up. Grub went down to the little stream and gathered water, then poured it over the mound. When it was finished he looked around; maybe a dozen of these trees had his friends and family buried beneath them. Now he and Nana were the only ones left.

Won't forget.

Grub and Nana went out taking together most times, now. Grub was worried he'd come back and she'd be gone too, and he'd be all alone. So they waited by the little dirt road, where the big people in their big, moving shinies sometimes came along, spewing their black smoke that burned Grub's nose. They'd put things in the road, sharpened sticks and bones that made the big shinies slow down or stop, and then when the big people got out to see what was wrong, Grub or Nana or both of them would come out of the woods and take.

They took more in the few weeks following Bother's death than they had in the months leading up to it. It made Grub feel better, or at least it kept him occupied.

It also made him careless. He was less concerned about being seen now; before he could only remember a few times any of the big people spotted him, and how they'd scream, how they'd get back in their big shinies and wait, sometimes days, before trying to fix them and be on their way again. Now, they saw him more often than not. Grub didn't care. Nana still stayed hidden, but Grub just didn't care. Let them look. After all, the big people made them.

One afternoon, when the sky was cloudy and the air was cold, they set up a sharpened deer bone in the dirt on the big path. They waited, throwing glances at each other across the road, and finally, Grub heard the loud groan of one of the big people's big shinies. He crouched in waiting. The ground rumbled a little, and the bone fell over.

Nana came out of the woods to set it upright, and then the big shiny came, faster than most.

"Nana!" Grub shouted. To Grub's horror, she stopped what she was doing and looked up at him. He tried to shout, and instead shook his head, and then the big shiny slammed into Nana with a loud crunch. It bobbed as it rolled over her, sending her skidding along the road behind it. Dirt flew into the air as it came to a stop, with Nana's crumpled body a few feet behind it.

Two big people got out of the big shiny.

"The fuck was that?"

"Look. God, it's some kind of animal. Like a mangy raccoon. It's gross."

"Not gross!" Grub shouted. He ran out of the woods on his hands and knees; he was always faster on all fours. The two big people stared at him in disgust and horror, and he stared back at them in disgust and rage. "Not gross! Nana!"

"What the fuck?" one of the big people shouted.

"It's a monster!" The other one cried as he practically dove back into the big shiny. The other followed, and the big shiny sped off, kicking up more dirt and rocks, half-burying Grub and Nana.

He had to un-bury her to bury her. He didn't cry this time, he only stood silent and cold. Winter would arrive soon, which meant less taking. Grub would need to stock up.

Grub spent all of his time taking. He ate little, he slept less. And every day, he was more hurt, more angry.

One day he set up his little bone in the road. A big shiny came bumbling along and ran over it. A loud pop followed, and the thing came to a halt. One of the big people got out, along with a small big person, not small like Grub, just smaller than the big ones. A young one.

"Stay in the car, honey," the big one said. "It's just a blown tire."

The small one was holding something, a fuzzy. It looked like the ones Grub sometimes saw out in the woods, only different, made to look more like the big people did. They were always making things in their own image like that.

Grub wanted it. He had to take it. Bother would've loved it, Nana would've slept beside it and cherished it more than any of their other shinies.

"Daddy," the small person said.

"What is—" The big person looked to where she was pointing. Grub realized she was pointing at him. He didn't care. He realized he was holding his sharpened bone. He didn't care. Grub just wanted to take. For Bother and Nana.

All of the pain and all of the rage came out as Grub drove the bone into the big person's gut. He had to reach upward to do it. The big person screamed, but not like his girl did. Warm red poured out, trickled along Grub's fingers. He didn't care.

"Please," the big person groaned. "Please!"

"Take," Grub said. He gestured at the girl's fuzzy. She looked down at it, ran forward, and thrust it toward Grub.

"Take it!" she shouted. "Just leave my daddy alone!"

Grub looked at the fuzzy. He yanked his bone out, and the big person fell to his knees. More red came out, spilled into the dirt, disappeared into it like Bother and Nana and all the others had. He looked from the fuzzy to the girl and back, then snatched it away. Red soaked into its fur.

The big person was lower to the ground now, his soft throat exposed. Grub looked at the bone in his hand, then the fuzzy in the other.

"Why..." the big person said.

"Never forget where we come from," Grub said. It would've been so easy to plunge the bone into the big person's throat. But Bother wanted Grub to remember, so Grub wanted the big people to remember, and he supposed you can't remember anything once you're dead.

"Wh—what?"

"Grub won't. Grub won't forget."

Clutching the fuzzy tight in his hand, Grub scampered off into the woods, ready for a long, cold winter.

Melonhead
by
Nick Brown

Purple. There were two of them on the little girl. I watched her walk with other humans, but I bet they wouldn't see me do it.

I clawed and scraped the white and red away to get to the purple. I held it in my mouth as I scampered from the dark, gray road, and back to my forest.

23

Out in the Woods
by
David J. Lovato

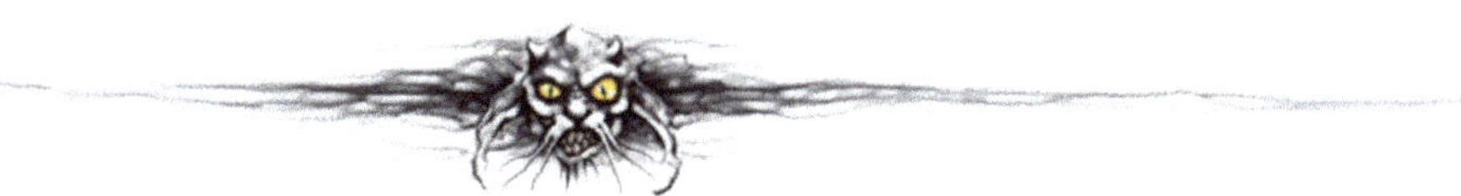

The following is a choose-your-own-adventure story. Certain sections will end with a choice, and guide you to a specific page depending on which choice you've made. The story may play out many different ways, so other pages should be ignored to avoid spoiling other paths.

If you find yourself lost, the hands will guide you.

"Put the book down."

Jessie lowered her book and saw her friends staring at her. She blushed, slid her bookmark into its place, and closed the book. "Sorry, guys. It's getting good."

"It's fine," Andy said.

"It's not fine," Mark said. "It's rude as hell."

The tension was as thick as the air. It wasn't hot, but walking among the ups and downs of the woods took effort. All the more reason Jessie shouldn't be reading while walking, she supposed.

"Anyway," Steph said. "Which way is it?"

They had walked until the paths and trails dwindled to little more than gaps between trees that were slightly wider than other gaps between trees, and Jessie was pretty sure it shouldn't have taken this long to get to the supposed fire pit. Now two of those paths branched out ahead of them, spaces hiding among spaces between trunks that had been there since before any of the teens were born.

"That's why I wanted everyone paying attention," Mark replied. He glared Jessie's way.

Jessie shrugged. "I've never even been to this thing."

"It's your place, Mark," Melissa said. "Shouldn't you know how to get to it?"

Mark looked around. "It's more my brother's. I've only been out to it once or twice."

John slung his bag to the ground; everyone else was carrying supplies, but he had a whole tent.

Mark got his phone out and opened his GPS app. "I told you you didn't need to bring that."

John shrugged. "Never know when it'll rain."

"Well?" Steph asked.

"Shut up," Mark replied. "It's really hard to tell, look. Kinda looks like both ways will get us there."

Everyone took turns looking at Mark's phone over his shoulder. He had zoomed all the way in, but the satellite image had been taken in the spring or summer, when the trees were full of leaves, and the little blue arrow marking their current position and direction was the only bearing they had. Now the trees were naked and lifeless, save for the occasional thin branches swaying in the wind. The sky above them was turning white; no satellite pictures would be taken today.

Ahead, the two paths waited. The one to the left looked somewhat like an actual trail, the right path looked more like a slightly wider gap between trees than anything else.

"Well, I'm tired of standing around," John said. He stretched, then picked up the tent and slung it back around his shoulders. "We still have to set up once we get there. So let's go."

For the left path, turn to page X1 (49).
For the right path, turn to page X2 (103).

Crypto Bizarro

Hagridden
by
David J. Lovato

The old hag goes by many names. In the Philippines it's called the Batibat, in Laos it's known as a dab tsuam, and in Old English they call it a maere, which is where we get the word "nightmare." But in all of these places, and under all these names, the story is the same.

You wake up suddenly, and you can't move. Well, sometimes you can move your eyes, but that's it. You're paralyzed. You can't even scream.

Sometimes she'll be at the foot of your bed. Sometimes she'll be watching you from the corner of the room. Sometimes there will be more than one, all standing around your bed, staring down at you. But usually, she'll be right on top of you, crouched or sitting or even standing right on your chest.

K hnbr ot kg xvr gkdvx pgs lph xvnlr xhn zraanhklv dakgxl, lnir ogbgnhg akdvx lnouqr urmarqxkgd nmm nm urxkgpl kg xvr spub. Jox k sng'x nhg p qpx.

Modern science calls it sleep paralysis, or SP. In early America they called it being "hagridden."

The hag isn't always involved, but SP is often accompanied by vivid hallucinations, like a lucid dream, or more like a lucid nightmare. If it happens with your eyes open, whatever you're staring at will often become part of these visions. That's how it was for me; I would just be lying in bed, unable to move even my eyes, powerless to make a sound. Sometimes I would see strange lights, and always I would feel a presence, something in the room just outside my field of vision, something that wanted me dead.

These are two types of SP: vivid hallucination SP, and evil presence SP. There's a third type though, and I haven't experienced that one before. I hope I never do, but my hope these days is running a little thin.

The topic came up one time, a few months ago, at my friend Steve's house. I don't remember how we got to talking about SP, but that's how it is with good friends; one topic just leads to another. He told me he had it often, almost every month, in fact. And his was almost always the third type: suffocation SP.

It's like the other kinds I brought up, only in addition to being unable to move, you can't breathe. According to legend, it's because of the hag sitting on your chest. Sometimes she collapses your lungs, sometimes she chokes you with her hands, and some will swear she just looks into your eyes and steals your breath.

Steve started having SP when he was young. At first it was mild, just an inability to move. As he got older he would sense something in the room with him, something small and far away. Month after month, year after year, it got closer, he said.

Then one night he saw it. He said he was propped up with his back against his headboard, because he had fallen asleep while reading. His book was on his chest, and it felt like it weighed a solid ton. He couldn't move as he stared at the foot of his bed, illuminated only slightly by moonlight coming in through the window. He felt that evil presence, for once coming from right ahead of him.

Then the darkness changed, like something even darker was moving into his line of sight. A small, round shadow started to rise from just past the bed, and when it stopped, to him it looked like a short, cloaked woman, barely taller than his bed.

The book on his chest pressed harder and harder into him, and he could barely breathe. Then he was suddenly awake. That's how it usually happens, you just snap out of it. There was nothing in his room, he could breathe fine, and the place even seemed a little less dark.

He told me she showed up again a few weeks later, but this time she was *on* the bed. She was small, like a child, and her cloak covered her face, all but a knobby chin. She just sat there, a few inches shy of his feet, while he struggled to move, struggled to breathe, struggled to at least peel his eyes from her.

The next time he saw her, he had again fallen asleep while reading. The book was touching his neck this time, and the hag was on top of his stomach. She weighed more than someone that size possibly could have, and the book felt like it was cutting into his skin. She reached forward and took the book, which was an immense weight off of him, and then she started to tear out the page he was on.

This time, when he woke up, it was daytime. He was alone again, sitting up as he had been, and his book was on the floor next to his bed. He reached down to pick it up, and when he did, a single torn page fell out of it and fluttered to the ground.

Needless to say, he stopped reading in bed. I told him he was being silly, but he also spent pretty much all of his savings on a camera, one with a motion sensor. He kept this plugged in all night and wore it around his neck like a necklace. A few times he caught pictures, but it was always just from him stirring in his sleep.

I woke up one morning to a phone call. It was Steve's mother, and she was in tears. She asked if I could come over, that's all I could make out of what she was saying, so I told her I'd be right there.

Steve had died in his sleep. It's called SUNDS, or "sudden unexpected nocturnal death syndrome." It's very rare, mostly affects young males, and is in essence a medical term for an otherwise healthy person dying in their sleep for no reason.

Obviously I was grief-stricken, and Steve's mother was as well. She looked like she wanted to say something to me, but things kept coming up, people kept calling and asking questions. Soon that look she had slipped from my mind, but now I can't forget it.

A few days later I had another SP episode. It was the kind I normally have, the evil presence SP, but this one was different. It was more vivid, more real, and that feeling that something was just out of my line of sight was stronger than ever. The closest thing I can relate it to is when you blow a bubble and it gets so big that there's one moment you just know it's about to pop. And then it does.

At Steve's wake his mother pulled me aside. She told me he had been sleeping with a camera around his neck. This was nothing new to me, but then she told me it had taken a picture, and according to the coroner, it must have been taken right before he died. The police had searched thoroughly, there was no doubt at all that he had died of SUNDS, with no sign of foul play, so they passed the picture off as nothing. A camera anomaly. Steve's mother showed me the picture, and asked if I had any idea what it was.

I told her I didn't. I don't really feel like it was a lie, because I *don't* know what it was. But I do know what it looked like: A gnarly old woman, shrouded in darkness, with a knobby chin, an ecstatic grin, and bulging, staring eyes. The kind of eyes that could stop your breath.

I have a lot on my mind, and I still haven't put Steve's death behind me. But I just can't shake this feeling that I'm never really alone anymore.

I tried sleeping with the light on, but I soon realized that only makes it easier to see, so it makes me feel more vulnerable. I tried bringing my dog to bed with me, and even though she used to sleep at the foot of my bed every night, she won't stay anymore. If I shut the door, she just sits at it, scratching and barking until I let her out.

It's so hard for me to sleep. I know any night now that bubble is going to break, and I'll see the top of a hood start to peek up from the foot of my bed. I don't know what I'll do then. What *can* I do? There's no such thing as monsters, everybody knows that. And yet I wonder how something that doesn't exist can be described by different cultures in different places at different times, always the same story, just with a different name.

Maybe that's what bothers me so much: It all comes down to a different name, which makes it so easy to write it off. To me it was murder, but they called it SUNDS. They call it sleep paralysis, but I'm being hagridden. And when they find me dead in my sleep the same way they found Steve, they'll call it a coincidence.

I don't feel like going alone into the dark. I've decided that when she comes for me, I won't look away. When she stares at me, I'll stare back. Maybe if I see her coming, she can't hurt me. Maybe if we all see her coming, she'll go away forever.

Crypto Bizarro

33

Jon's Folly
by
Josh Leichliter

Jon was a pauper
Jon had no penny
for penance he owed
well Jon counted twenty

one for a lie
two more for grinning
three for a laugh
at least four more for sinning

five would be had
for the sixth time he begged
but seven more favors
saw eight people dead

nine times he cried
for ten that they buried
eleven life terms
from twelve on the jury

Jon was convicted
poor Jon would be dead
the favors he owed
worth more than his head

Jon was just thirteen
fourteen on the fence
'twas fifteen more hours
til his sixteenth offense

seventeen lashes
with an eighteen foot whip
left nineteen bones broken
and twenty more split

Jon reg**r**ets lying
Jon la**m**ents sin
for pen**a**nce he owed
he paid wi**t**h his skin

Shall we begin again?

37

What's in the Attic?
by
David J. Lovato

On a separate sheet of paper, make a list from 1-26. Then, come up with words for each of the following, and insert them into the story on the next page.

1. Male's name
2. Body part
3. Noun
4. Vehicle
5. Adjective
6. Adjective or Feeling
7. Adverb
8. Adjective ending with –ly
9. Color
10. Sound Effect
11. Saying or Proverb
12. Hobby or Activity
13. Number between 1 and 12
14. Name of a loved one or close friend
15. Weapon
16. Name of a room that isn't the Attic
17. Name of another loved one or close friend
18. Name of a specific place (state, country, province, etc.)
19. The same weapon as #15
20. Last name
21. Same loved one as #17
22. Horror adjective
23. Color
24. Body part
25. Something you'd find in a kitchen
26. Organ

You inherited the house from your great uncle 1.______, after he died of a ruptured 2.______. Nobody told you that the old house on 3._____ Tree Lane was the only one around for miles. As you pulled up to it in your 4.______, a tingle went up your spine. Clouds covered the sun, the trees shook with the 5.______ breeze—one you couldn't even feel.

"It's nothing," you said. "I'm just 6.______ because it's a new house."

A long path led among the leafless trees, snaking its way through the lifeless grass. You walked up 7.______, feeling more uneasy with every step. Then—what was that? Did something move in the upstairs window?

Impossible. Anyway, the windows were too grimy to see through from down here. You pressed on, reaching the old wooden steps that led up to the door. Each groaned 8.______ as you stepped on it, threatening to break beneath you.

You found respite on the front porch. It was late in the afternoon, and you took a last look at your 9.______ vehicle, offering to give you a ride out of this creepy place. Instead you turned and tried the knob. It was locked, not that anyone would have any reason to come way out here, let alone try to break in. You had the key, which slid roughly into the lock. It made a 10.______ sound as you turned it, then the door popped open.

The lights came on when you flicked the switch, and though they were dim, you already felt better about the place. The old man's furniture still adorned it, and the house looked recently cleaned, if only lightly. Dust settled in the spaces where the floor met the walls, and on top of old ceiling fans.

"11._______," you reminded yourself, then got to work settling in. After a few hours of 12.______, the uneasiness had completely passed. With a violent yawn, you decided to turn in for the first night in your new home.

At 13._____ o'clock in the morning, you heard a sound. It stirred you from a dream about 14.______ calling to you for help, so your heart was already pounding. A few seconds dragged by like molasses; you wondered if you'd actually heard anything, and then you heard it again: shuffling, like footsteps.

You grabbed the 15.______ from beside the night stand, then stood up. More shuffling sounds, coming from the 16._______. "Who's there?" You called.

Through the crack in the door, a figure moved. How could something get all the way to the hall so quickly? Your eyes must've been playing tricks on you. Cautiously, you opened your bedroom door... and nothing happened. No sounds, no movement.

Until the attic door slammed shut.

You raced up the stairs, weapon in hand, and tried the knob, but it was locked. Strange, that door only locks with a key. You felt a sudden fear and turned, but there was nothing.

You investigated the set of keys you'd been left, and discovered there was no attic key. It wasn't even listed in the paperwork describing everything your uncle left you. He must not have had a key to leave.

Still a little shaken, you slept with your bedroom door shut and locked.

The next day went by without anything unusual happening. You even got a call from 17.______ all the way in 18.________. The two of you talked for hours, and before you knew it, it was nighttime. You said your goodnights. You were in the kitchen making a late night snack when movement caught your eye. You whipped around to face a small vent in the wall above a little cubby door, but saw only a light cobweb drifting with the air conditioner. You chuckled at how silly you were, then went on to finish your meal.

That night, you heard noises, this time coming from the kitchen. You reached for your trusty 19.______, and then scoured your house, but you didn't find anything. Only the attic remained unsearched.

Shaking, you called the police. They seemed annoyed by the prospect of driving all the way out there, but eventually sent someone out. It took an hour to arrive. Officer 20.______ searched your house and found nothing. Yawning, the officer asked "What's in the attic?"

"I don't know," you said. "I don't have a key."

The officer grunted, clearly annoyed. "I can make a copy of the lock and get you a key by next week. Other than that, I think we're done here. You enjoy your night."

Nothing stirred the rest of the night. You felt safe, even a little happy that you'd finally get your attic key. Smiling, you went to sleep.

A few uneventful days went by, then you were awoken again one night. You reached for your weapon—but it was gone.

By now you were more annoyed than scared. You found a baseball bat in the closet, took it in hand, and headed downstairs, toward the sound.

You turned on the kitchen light. The baseball bat clattered to the floor as you used both hands to cover your mouth. On the table was a clean white plate, serving up 21._______'s freshly severed head.

Your phone was all the way in your bedroom, on the night stand. And anyway, the police were an hour away. You reached for the baseball bat, but it was gone.

Tap. Tap.

Wood on metal. Slowly, so slowly, you turned toward the vent you'd noticed the other day. The cubby below it was wide open, and sitting inside was a 22.______ man, or woman, or *thing*. It had desaturated 23.______ skin, straw-like hair, and was missing a 24.________. It was tapping your baseball bat against the vent. And it was *smiling* at you.

You turned to run, but didn't make it a single step before you felt the blow on the back of your head. You fell, turning, and landed on your back, looking up at the 25.________. Pain ravaged your body and you screamed as the thing's long, slender fingers tore into you and ripped out your 26.________.

In a daze of pain and darkness, you felt yourself being dragged around the house, like the thing was giving you a tour. Up the stairs you went, the thing carrying you by one foot, your head bumping against every stair.

"And thisssss here is the aaaaattic," the creature said. It opened the door with a simple turn of the knob, then threw you inside. You slid across the hard, dusty wood floor, trailing blood the whole way, and came to rest in the middle of the room.

The creature entered the attic and shut the door behind it. You heard it lock. Then you remembered something almost funny:

The police would come by with your attic key in the morning.

As prey we graze, and as predators, stalk

Boustrephedon
by
Josh Leichliter

I am pretty.

?ees yeht t'naC

I walk around the park sometimes, at night. I hope to meet someone who will agree with me. Like that one, he's handsome!

.mih hctac I tub ,won tsaf gninnur s'eH .mih wollof I

"Am I pretty?" I ask.

!mih etah I !taht etah I .suoedih m'I skniht eH !deracs skool eH !gnimaercs s'eH.

"Tell me I'm pretty."

.eromyna emosdnah ton s'eh won ,dam yllear tog I

I just want someone to tell me I'm pretty.

.ytterp ma I

Can't they see?

one claws my back, the other my heart

Wych Elm
by
Josh Leichliter

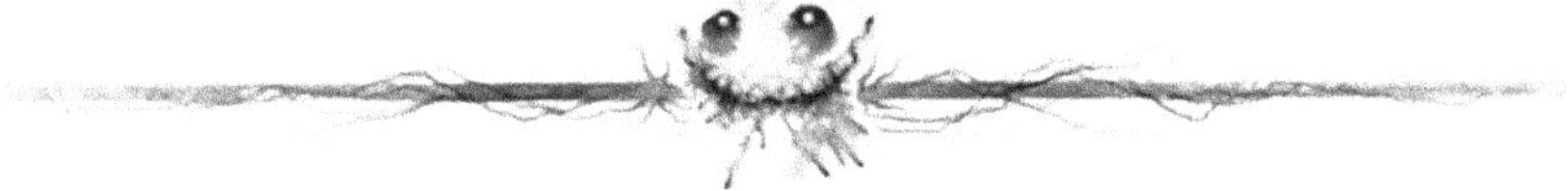

Abella tripped and crashed hard into the ground, smacking her chin on a rock. Half-dazed and bleeding, she flailed like a dying jackrabbit as the malevolent forest stabbed at her with wooden talons.

Soaked in blood and desperate for breath, she managed to find footing and stumbled forward. The thick brambles tore at her skin and hair as she barreled through them. The wicked trees only seemed to thicken as she attempted her escape. She trudged with all her might to gain precious ground.

Like a fly in a web, she was captured in the tangled claws of this possessed forest. Constricting her like a snake, all hope escaped with her last breaths. She spat her last words, addled with frantic nuance only the dying can muster. "I... found you," she gasped as the knotted limbs constricted an inch further. "...Palyngrae." One more inch, then Abella exhaled for the last time.

Roman stared in disbelief. The innocence of his young age spoiled at the sight of it: Twisted, inhuman, and puppet-like, red liquid flowed through its cracks and joints and ran down the petrified flesh of its spindly twig legs. Its eyes glistened wet with the fading sunlight.

He knew those eyes. He had found his beloved big sister. Roman wept as he tried to free her from her coffin of twisted green limbs. Fluid gushed as he clawed at the bark and vines that tethered Abella, spraying his face with an acrid mixture of sap and blood.

Screaming in fear and defeat, Roman fell to her rooted feet, his own hands bleeding from the futile struggle. Tears rained from his eyes, realizing that he couldn't save her.

"I'll get help Abella, I'll be back, I promise!" Roman spun on his heels and bolted forward. A crackling sound erupted as the forest exploded around him, pelting him with wooden shrapnel. Dazed, he lifted his head and turned to see his once-sister standing fiercely over him, her green eyes flickering in the dark. A dozen broken, jagged tree limbs aimed at him, poised like scorpions ready to strike.

"Dad!" Roman screamed before he was skewered by the slithering limbs of his former sister.

***

Bill crashed onto the scene, saw Roman on the ground, and the impossible thing on top of him. He instinctively opened fire with his hunting rifle, striking the Wych Elm twice in the chest and head. Whip-like vines lashed out from the foliage around him, ripping Bill to pieces. The forest came alive and massacred the remaining fifteen members of the search party, painting the trees a glistening red.

***

The forgotten forest god Palyngrae was delighted by this centennial's tribute. The acting, the script, the screams, all were excellent. He had laid the seeds, and the drama had blossomed beautifully. The pact was completed, though the benefactors had been long forgotten. Palyngrae was no longer called upon it seemed, but he was still eager to collect. To him, a contract was a contract.

Satisfied, his normal sacrifice of ten (one for each decade of the hundred), had been exceeded by eight, almost double. The elms lavished in the blood spilled, and their thirst was tamed. For now. This new prey looked and tasted different, but was to his liking. Feeling lazy and sated, Palyngrae dozed and dreamt dark, autumnal dreams.

Aeh gv essigsyvg
sv jues fviz nlxa
yg sur gyfus, iizs
ys stbg ysz
essigsyvg sv hvt.

Out in the Woods
(Continued from page 26 X1)

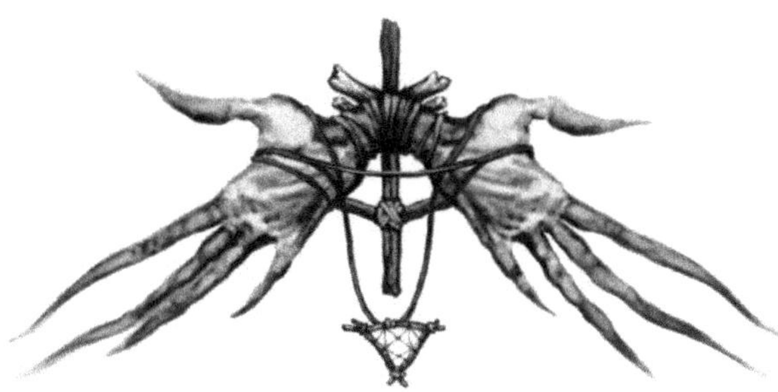

John started down the path to the left. He got no protests from his friends, who followed single file, leaves crunching beneath their boots and All-Stars. After a few seconds, Steph fell in beside Jessie.

"Hey," she said. "Sorry my brother is such a dick."

"It's okay," Jessie said.

"He's just mad because he can't find the place. He's excited, really. It's a really cool little place."

Jessie hadn't known Steph or Mark long; she knew Andy and Melissa, and knew the others through them. She'd only ever seen John around at school. As quiet as he'd been this whole hike, that didn't surprise her at all.

The six teens in their abandoned woods crept a few more minutes across their own little patch of time. Suddenly, Mark stood up straighter. "There it is!" He started off faster, and the others followed. Even John made like the tent weighed nothing.

The clearing was barely a clearing; the trees had been steadily pressing in, but here they relaxed for a fifteen-foot radius, near the center of which was a ring of stones. The remains of long burned-out fires rested within, and a few good burning logs and branches were stacked nearby. Jessie could see clear spots on the ground, probably where sleeping bags once lay, and here and there was an empty beer bottle.

Steph picked one of these up. "Fucking Tommy. I'm telling Mom and Dad."

"Forget him," Mark said. "Tonight this place is ours."

Mark and Andy headed into the trees around the clearing to gather more firewood. Melissa set her bag down beside a fallen trunk, which she sat on. John started quietly setting up some chairs.

"You want some help with that?" Jessie asked.

He looked up at her. The hike had made him sweaty, which made his glasses slide down his nose a little when he looked down. He pushed them back up his face. "Sure. It's not hard."

Steph came over to help as well, and they had the site set up before Mark and Andy returned with armfuls of firewood.

"Thanks for nothing," Steph said to Melissa.

Melissa cracked her neck. "Welcome, babe."

Steph lurched forward and tickled her sides. Melissa shrieked and both laughed, the sounds echoing across the trees only to die off seconds later. They really were on their own out here.

The sky turned darker while work turned into play. The heat from the fire had them all take off their jackets, and conversations echoed or vanished among the trees.

Jessie, however, didn't feel carefree. She laughed, told stories, and made jokes with the others, enjoying their company and getting to know new friends, but she felt an uneasiness she couldn't quite shake.

"You all right?" John asked.

"Yeah, you're being awful quiet," Andy said. "Even quieter than him." He nodded at John. John smiled and flipped Andy off.

"Just a little creeped out, I guess. Never really been out in the woods before."

"We should tell scary stories!" Andy said. His smile faded. "I mean, unless you don't want to, Jessie."

"No, it's fine," Jessie said. "I love stories!"

"I don't know if I'm into this," Melissa said.

"You spook easy?" Mark asked.

Melissa shrugged. "Not right now. But later, when y'all fall asleep and I'm the last one up?"

The group laughed together, but the season and the setting caught up to them, and before long they were taking turns looking up and reading scary stories on their phones.

John was getting really into a story he was telling when Jessie felt a chill break over her. Even the fire seemed to dim. She rubbed her arms and leaned into Andy. He flinched at first, but then relaxed.

"You okay?" he whispered.

"I feel cold suddenly. No big deal."

Andy leaned into her a little. It was nice. Jessie knew he liked her, and probably had for a long time. She didn't mind; she kind of liked him, too.

Mark was the first to bust out his sleeping bag, and the others followed suit. Nobody knew who fell asleep first, just that it was someone else's turn to tell a story, but out in the dark in their little clearing, they were falling asleep. Scary tales turned into soft goodnights, followed by the quiet of the woods.

Jessie woke to the sound of a twig cracking, leaves rustling. She ignored it at first, drifting on the edge of sleep, and then sat up suddenly. Had she heard something else? Had she dreamed it? She looked around, but it was too dark to see anything but the coals of the fire, or the stars above, here and there slashed out of existence by the branches of the trees.

Jessie lay back down. She wondered what time it was, and checked her phone: 1:44. She sat back up. That couldn't be right; it would mean she'd only been asleep for ten, fifteen minutes. She slid her finger across the screen to unlock her phone, but the lock screen only wiggled slightly and wouldn't budge. She held the power button to try to turn it off, but nothing happened.

Something felt wrong. It was that feeling from earlier in the night, the unease, like the trees were watching her. She desperately hoped one of her friends hadn't fallen asleep yet, and looked from dark shape to dark shape, hoping to see someone sitting up. None were.

Leaves crunched, this time closer to the clearing. In the small spaces where moonlight broke through, Jessie could see a light fog covering the ground. Her heart beat faster. If it were just the noises or just the phone, she'd probably dismiss it and go back to sleep, but she was genuinely worried. She decided to wake one of her friends.

To wake Melissa, turn to page X1-2 (89).
To wake Andy, turn to page X1-3 (64).

Trapped
by
David J. Lovato

can't move. can'T even think. thinking in circles, everything in circles. going around and around, spinning, so dizzy now—throwing up. throwing up what? empty stomach. thRowing that up, that's it. inside out. upside-down. turning around now, watching my guts come out. out to play, rainy day. nothing left to sAy. tongue tied, stomach in knots. darkness is all i've got. tear my heart from my chest, no one ever taught me how to Part with it. there be monsters here, you know they're there but you can't see clear—did you hear? something in the darkness, something that shouldn't exist. sPlit my skin when i clench my fists, feel it tear me limb from limb. then do it again, every single day re-live this. tomorrow, today, yesterday, all the same. over and over again. nothing but pain. no respite, here there is no light. no sight, no mind, only everything breaking mine. out of time, out of life, even though i'm not really alive. spidErs crawl over my eyes. time drops me off here, then flies. like the ones gathered around some bloody, festering thing—that's me. anD it always will be, because I

The Dark
by
Nick Brown

<u>Day 1</u>

The dark isn't the problem. The silence is. I can't tell what happened. My mind races as I think of hands or arms or slimy somethings grabbing me after getting home from school.
I fell back to sleep. I remember Jon could drink way more than me, and I've always thought I was a light weight.
The darkness is oppressive. It's like hiding in the closet playing hide-and-seek. I can't move much. I thought I saw light a little while ago, but it just ended up being stars in my eyes. My head hurts so badly. Fuzzy.
It's been at least 5 hours. I thought I heard people, but after listening for a while, I realized it was a highway.
I didn't think I'd ever breathe again. So much dust keeps filtering into my prison.
I have to sleep.

<u>Day 2</u>

I thought I was sleeping, but I felt wet. I woke up and couldn't feel anything but dry desert dust. What is that sensation I feel? Doesn't even matter…
It happened again. I went to sleep and I felt wetness move around my body. My mind is dreaming of snakes and other creepy-crawly things.
I fell asleep again.

<u>Day 3</u>

I've been feeling around. I'm in what seems like a coffin.
No.
It's been days since I could write. I'm weak. I keep hearing sounds. Cars? TV? What?
Water is coming in. From above! It's filling my coffin. I desperately sip for air from the ceiling of my tomb. I can't believe this is it. My life.
I held my breath after all the water filled my box. I felt the rush of water down my throat, I opened my eyes. I saw black tendrils pulling me down into the murk.

<u>Day 4</u>

It was nice. Subtle. But when I awoke in a different land, I was pushed into a coffin underground and I was trapped again. I screamed as long as I could until I went to sleep.

Out in the Woods
(Continued from page 138 X2-2-2)

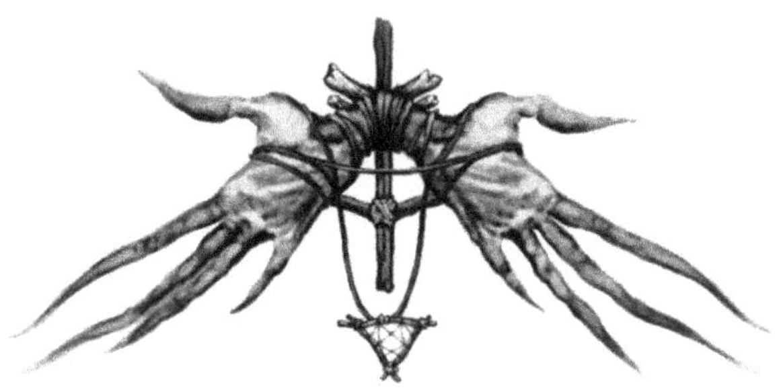

"We can't leave them," Jessie said.

"Yeah," Andy replied. The trio turned and headed back into the trees.

"John! Melissa!" Steph cried. The woods were silent; not even her voice echoed.

"John!" Andy screamed. "Melissa!"

All was quiet and still.

Sploosh. Cold water surged up Jessie's leg.

"It's the creek."

"Follow it," Steph said. "It goes right by the campsite. Maybe we'll find John and Melissa."

The flashlight bounced among the trees, casting slender shadows along the ground. Jessie never held the light still, in fear that the creature would appear somewhere in the darkness.

They didn't find the campsite; instead the creek grew wider until it drained into a small, shallow lake.

"Melissa! John!"

No answer.

"Maybe we should go try to get help," Steph said.

Tendrils of fog broke across the water. The sound of static filled their ears.

Children. Come to Mother.

"You guys hear that, right?" Jessie asked.

"She's calling," Steph replied.

Come home.

"Ignore her," Jessie said. Andy kneeled down, opened his backpack, and started putting rocks inside it.

"Andy, what are you doing?"

"She's calling."

Jessie turned. Steph was waist-deep in the lake. Bony white tentacles shot out of the water, silent, and then Steph disappeared in a cloud of red dust. It pitter-pattered on the water, and then the night was silent and still.

"Andy..." Jessie said. She was filling her pockets with rocks. She didn't even remember moving.

Andy was wading into the lake, the bag of stones holding him down. His head disappeared under the water. A few seconds later, a huge bubble broke the surface. In the glow of the moonlight, Jessie could see the water was red. She was up to her chest in the lake now.

"Fuck you," Jessie said.

It's okay, child. Let Mother bring you home.

Jessie couldn't even close her eyes to shut out the frigid water. Darkness filled her sight, the world went silent except for the sound of static. Then a lighter black appeared, bony and gaunt, writhing under the water, reaching for her, ending her.

Death's Robe
by
Seth Thomas

Elliot heard the sound of trains pulling in and out of the station. He sat quietly with a notebook open to the third page, which was halfway full of doodles of varying size and shading. Some were quite simple, like a little man waving out at the viewer. Some were much more complex and seemed to jump off the page, reaching with whatever appendage the drawing was given. On one page was a mangy-looking old man. He looked like he was missing patches of skin, and his clothes were loose and torn. He reached forward, attempting to grab at whatever he could find with a hand that was missing some fingers.

Elliot worked on a different drawing as he waited for his train. It was a piece he had put at least two hours into; every pencil scratch, every smudge meant something. This wasn't just for his entertainment, it was for the person who'd stolen his heart, and nothing would stop him from finishing this masterpiece. Her name was Beth, and her birthday was a few days away.

On the page was an abandoned city, void of cars and people. The sky was colorful. It was not a rainbow, but more like a child had been painting with several different colors and had mixed them all together. The buildings were gloomy and decrepit. It was a dark but beautifully stark image he'd seen in his head many times before, and he just had to put it down on paper. Beth liked dark things like this, and she liked Elliot most of all.

The train station was a small and very old one in the heart of Centre County, Pennsylvania. The wooden bench below Elliot once gleamed with a fresh coat of red paint, but now it was faded and cracked and falling off. A train pulled up in front of it, shrieking as it slowed. A few moments of dull laughter and chatter passed Elliot by without him noticing anything but the city.

The noise caught up to him after some time, and he pulled his ticket from his pocket, then looked at the clock that hung on the wall to the right. Its wide, metal exterior was decades old, and the paint was starting to crack off of it as well. The glass plating was a dirty yellow, the fancy italic numbers beneath were barely legible. The old clock chimed at the quarter after mark as the train jerked into motion and exited the platform.

Elliot's train would not arrive for another hour. He smiled as he continued scraping his pencil over the paper's surface. The sky of the drawing had been finished at his home, it was an exact replica of the sky in his dream. He had sprayed it with a fixative spray to prevent the detail from smearing, so he could continue to work with peace of mind.

<hr>

A breeze picked up as Elliot worked on his drawing. He continued around the ruffling papers. Soon he was ready to change gears, so he pulled a duller pencil from his tattered bag. He loved the sound rounder-tipped pencils made against paper, and he used this one to pave the dark streets of the unpopulated city. As he went to fill in the white spaces that would be buildings, another train pulled in to the station.

Elliot looked up from his work, saw the old clock to his right, and chuckled at how fast time had gone by. He gathered all his drawing supplies together, then stood up to watch the train pull up to the platform. People began filtering in from other waiting areas. They crowded him, and he grew uncomfortable for the first time since he'd gotten on the train platform.

Scanning down the track at the next few cars of the train, Elliot moved forward with the teeming crowd, clutching his bag close to his chest. He looked up and saw the blue cloudless sky, then stepped up the stairs and into the train. Elliot shuffled toward the back, and found his seat on the second-to-last car. It was a window seat, Elliot's favorite. He could ride for hours and watch the scenery pass him by. He often drew what he saw.

<hr>

Elliot pulled out his city drawing and stared at it for a little while. Not long after he'd settled in, the conductor came by with a hole punch.

"Sir, may I please see your ticket?" The man's mustache twitched as he spoke. Elliot nodded and gave his ticket to the conductor, who punched a hole in it and passed it back to him. "Thank you, sir. We'll be departing shortly. I do hope you enjoy the ride." The older gentleman smiled; there was a small glint in his eye that bothered Elliot just a little bit, but he smiled back and gave a simple "Thank you."

The conductor called over a loud speaker for everyone to board. Elliot began to work on his drawing again, and before he knew it, the train was moving.

Between strokes of his pencils Elliot heard the sound of a squeaky trolley, and the sweet, alluring voice of the stewardess running it. It wasn't long until she made her way to Elliot.

Without her even saying anything, Elliot looked up from his drawing and smiled. The woman's face had a hint of familiarity to it, perhaps it was her auburn hair. She looked professional in her neatly-pressed uniform. She reminded Elliot of Beth.

"Sir, can I interest you in something from the trolley?"

Elliot marveled at the near infinite selection of food and drink on the two shelves of the bronze-plated cart. He ordered a beer and a submarine sandwich with turkey and lettuce. The woman walked past Elliot, asking the people behind him if they fancied something. Elliot's attention returned to his dark but colorful-skied city as the world outside passed him by.

It was not long before the quiet chatter of the passengers and the steadfast clacking of the wheels rolling down the tracks lulled Elliot toward sleep. He set his pencils away, covered his drawings, and leaned back in his seat.

Soon Elliot woke from his nap and looked out the window next to him. It was dark out, pitch black in fact, but the world was often illuminated by jagged daggers of lightning. Some stretched across the entire sky. Heavy winds blew the trees; it was pouring. The lights on the train began flickering.

Someone screamed. It was a woman, but Elliot couldn't see anything ahead of him, so he looked at the spot directly to his left. The person who once sat in the seat there had disappeared while he slept. There was nothing but a red stain in the seat.

In the seat across the aisle was a vague, bloody mass. The lights flickered out entirely, leaving Elliot in the dark, but a bolt of lightning hit awful close to the traincar; it illuminated the space long enough to give Elliot a clear view of what occupied the two seats: The lower half of a young woman. Her spine poked out through her torso cavity. Torn flesh and bloody remains of a sweater hung limp over the lower half of the torso. Some of the woman's intestines had spilled out and fallen to the floor. They bounced with every clack of the train's wheels. Above the seat was a handrail, and from it hung some of the entrails. They swung violently to the right as the train took a strong curve.

"What the fuck?"

Elliot nearly vomited. He saw that almost every surface had blood smeared on it. The train appeared to be void of any life, save for the sound of that trolley. This time, it squealed more than before, and in a lower pitch. The lights came back on, but they still flickered frequently.

The stewardess came with the trolley, and there was a cool aura surrounding her as she came closer. She was beautiful, just like before, even in this horrific setting. She looked back and forth at all the carnage, asking empty seats if they wanted anything more from the trolley. Her expression was sickeningly blithe. She asked the bifurcated woman to Elliot's left if she wanted anything, paused, and then cocked her head toward Elliot. He wanted to get up and run away, but his feet were stuck to the train floor. It was like pulling out of quicksand. She was blocking his way out, anyway. He didn't stand a chance.

"I'll take your flesh if you are finished, sir."

Elliot's eyes widened, his heart dropped. "Excuse me?"

"I will take that trash if you are finished, sir." The stewardess pointed to the sandwich wrapper in Elliot's lap. He handed it to her with shaky hands and noticed the apron she was wearing was splattered with blood. Her auburn hair now lay flat and dark and ragged, her neatly-pressed uniform was torn. Her skin was gray, the same as her eyes. She continued to smile as she tossed the trash into a bag hanging from the trolley.

"Is there anything else I can get you, sir?" She pursed her lips for a moment, and then flashed another smile, this time with two gleaming rows of pointed teeth. She waited for an answer, but Elliot was frozen with fear. He couldn't move, even as she opened her mouth wide, wider than any human should be able to, lurched forward, and clamped her mouth down on his side.

Elliot screamed as a huge portion of his skin, muscle, and inner organs fell out of his torso; some of it was hanging out of the stewardess's mouth. She opened and closed as her razor-sharp teeth and ground it up. Elliot clamped his hands over the gaping hole in his body, then fell limp against the window. He breathed heavily for a moment, and then closed his eyes.

When he opened them again, he realized he no longer heard the train or the screams. The lights were dim in what was now his room as he lay in his bed. Shuffling feet grabbed Elliot's attention. A fuzzy silhouette appeared in the doorway; he hadn't remembered leaving the bedroom door open.

Elliot sat up. His palms were sweating, and he called out to the figure. It fidgeted and began shambling across the room. Elliot quickly grabbed the gun off his nightstand and aimed for the head.

"Answer me, or I'm going to shoot!"

"Rehhhhh!"

Elliot pulled the trigger, but it only clicked.

"Shit!" He spied some ammunition on the table where the gun had been, and frantically began loading. The creature got very close and lurched forward, grabbing Elliot and pushing forward on him. He dropped the gun in the struggle, and the creature was dangerously close to getting a bite in. She was a female, and long, dark hair was hanging scraggly below her shoulders. She shoved forward and sank her teeth into Elliot's neck, ripping back some flesh. Blood poured like a faucet.

Elliot pushed on the woman with both hands, and her grip loosened and she fell backward. She made a loud thud when her back hit the hardwood floor. He picked up the gun, finished reloading, then got down on the floor, crouching above her. Elliot pressed the gun against her forehead. Lightning lit up the room. He saw her auburn hair, matted down from the rain.

With tears welling up, Elliot did what he had to: He fired one bullet into his fiancée's head. Elliot let out one quick sob, as sudden as a sneeze, and then fell limp to the ground. He leaned against the wall with the gun in one hand, and his other hand over the wound to stop the bleeding. Then he pressed the barrel of the gun to his temple, but couldn't pull the trigger.

I must be dreaming this.

Eventually, Elliot got up, weakly, and turned on the light. He grabbed his notebook and opened it to his latest work. The half-finished drawing of the dark city stared up at him, mocking him: You're not going to finish me.

Elliot moved the pencil across the drawing, but he was quickly growing more sluggish. He wanted to finish the drawing before it was too late. Hope became more lost to him as the minutes passed.

While Elliot made his desperate marks on the page, he remembered what had happened the night before: He and Beth were together when things went south, and people on the block began changing. As news came in that anyone bitten changed too, he and Beth tried to block every entrance. Despite their efforts, there was a breach. The attackers forced their way in through a door in the basement. In the end, one of them had gotten to Beth, despite how desperately he tried to prevent it.

He had built a pyre in the yard, but he had a present to finish. Beth's birthday was just a few days away. He thought he could finish it in time to burn it with her, but he must've fallen asleep.

As Elliot worked now, he began to drift off, this time not into sleep, but something else. He felt he was losing control of his body. After a short time, Elliot dropped the pencil on the paper. It rolled away, and clicked as it hit the floor. Blood dripped from the side of Elliot's hand, where it was running from the bite wound. It fell down onto the drawing, smudging some of the softer pencil strokes.

Elliot could have sworn he heard the faint fluttering of Death's robe in the distance as all of what he was began to take flight like a flock of birds. He groaned as he slowly headed for the door, and his wound continued to bleed. He didn't feel the pain anymore, but he was losing too much blood, and would probably not make it to the front door of his house before Death arrived. The city just lay there, unfinished on the floor, blood soaking into the pages, growing very cold.

Out in the Woods
(Continued from page 51 X1-3)

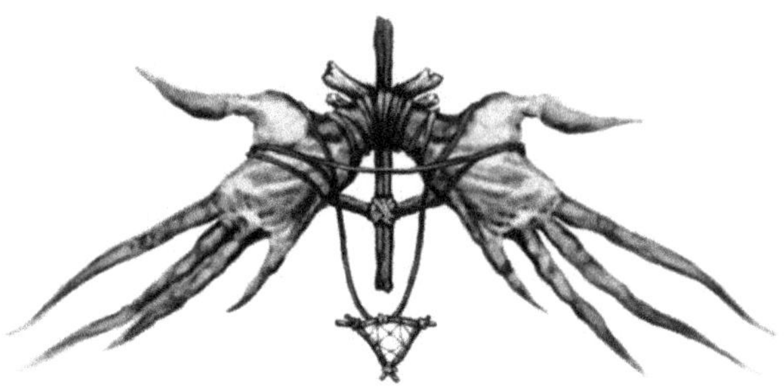

Jessie headed for Andy's sleeping bag and gently shook him. "Hey, Andy."

Andy stirred, then sat up. "Jessie? What's up?"

"Look, my phone's being weird."

Jessie showed him her phone. "I don't know, I just have this really bad feeling, like something is really, really wrong."

Andy checked his own phone and noticed the same thing. He looked around, then shouted, "Hey, guys! Get up!"

Jessie flinched; she hadn't expected him to just wake everyone like that, but as the others stirred, swearing and clearly angry, she felt better.

"Look at your phone. Can anyone get in?"

Anger turned to confusion. "Mine's not working," Steph said.

"Same here," Melissa said.

"Uh, guys? What the fuck is that?"

Mark was pointing out into the trees. John reached into his backpack and took out two flashlights. He tossed one to Mark, who turned it on and pointed it into the woods.

At the flashlight's edge, between the trees, barely even distinguishable from them, a woman at least eight feet tall stood. Her limbs were thin and long, her skin pale like bones, pulled so tight they might have been, cut through with deep ridges like tree bark.

"You gotta be fucking kidding me," Melissa said. "Which one of you assholes put that out there?"

A sound like rain mixed with rustling leaves bled into Jessie's ears, and the thing's skin moved up out of the ground, along its bones, and back into the ground behind it as it crept forward, growing along the ground instead of walking.

"Oh my God," Steph said.

Fog appeared, like it had already been there and just now thickened up. The creature was only a few feet away. Jessie rubbed at her eyes, but the fog persisted.

"Fucking run!" Mark screamed, and the teens bolted for the trees.

Jessie was pretty sure she was heading the way they'd originally come from, dodging trees and trying not to trip on roots or rocks. She turned to see Mark, Andy, and Steph following, but no sign of John or Melissa. She stopped running, and the others stopped shortly past her, leaving Jessie uncomfortably close to the darkness they were trying to escape.

"Why are we stopping?" Mark asked.

"Where are the others?"

Everyone looked around. "Shit," Andy said. "They must've gotten lost."

"We have to go back," Steph said.

"Toward that thing?"

"They'd come back for us." Steph turned to Jessie. "You're with me, right?"

To keep running, turn to page X1-3-1 (160).
To go back for the others, turn to page X1-3-2 (183).

The Hunger
by
David J. Lovato

Every year, toward the end of March, our town offers a free "Spring Cleaning" event, where they collect and haul off everyone's trash for free over the weekend. This is why my dad and I are in the basement storage room, poring over old boxes full of things like toys from when I was little, old documents, boxes of clothes forgotten so long, I don't even remember wearing them.

It's chilly for Spring, and I just want to get this over with. Luckily, the habit of waiting until the last minute to do anything runs in the family, and we're scrambling to get the last few bags of trash out before Spring Cleaning ends in a few hours.

I feel like we've made a big enough dent in our storage room, and at this point, I'm mostly looking at things I find interesting. That's when I notice the little brown cigar box tucked away behind a stack of records (Dad says we can't toss them, but we don't even own a record player).

"What's in here?" I ask.

Dad narrows one eye at the box, then he motions for me to hand it over. I do. He pops the latch and pulls out a small stack of old Polaroids.

"Old photos," he says. "Look, it's Grampa." He hands me a photo of his dad, and I'm surprised to see a young man who looks nothing like my grampa as I remember him. The man in the photo has long hair, and he's wearing leather and a tattered denim vest. He's leaning against the side of a store smoking a cigarette next to a sign that reads *No Smoking!*

"When was this?" I ask.

My dad shrugs. "Probably late 70s, early 80s. He was a bit of a metalhead. Still is, in some ways." Dad moves the picture to the bottom of the stack. The next photo shows an old car. It looks familiar.

"I've seen that car."

"Grampa still had it back when you were really little. He probably sold it not long after this photo. I'm surprised you remember it at all."

My desire to get the cleaning done has been replaced with curiosity. Now I'm standing next to my dad, who has taken a lean against a stack of old boxes, and we're going through the photos. If nothing else, it passes the time until we can call it quits.

"Here's Gramma," Dad says. I see a young woman I don't recognize. "She died when you were a baby." He doesn't seem too upset about it.

"I don't remember her at all."

"I don't expect you would. She was a good person. Strict, but good." Dad squints at the photo, lifts it up to get better lighting on it. "I really don't know when some of these were taken."

Meanwhile, I'm captivated and horrified by the next photo down. It's a dark photo, like the only light came from the flash of the camera. The picture is a close-up of someone's face, only it's not quite together; there's something terribly wrong with it. Then I realize that the person's face is literally splitting in two, revealing rough, red muscle beneath. The edges of the flesh are bound to metal, which is pulling apart like the teeth of a zipper. What intrigues me more than scares me is that the subject of the photo is clearly alive and in no pain—in fact, the person is smiling. As I stare I realize this isn't a happy smile; it looks hungry. It looks malicious.

"Dad, what's that?"

Dad turns his attention away from the photo of his mother. Suddenly he slaps the picture of Gramma over the creepy face. "Fuck," he says. He sighs deeply and shakes his head, then he pinches the bridge of his nose. He sighs again, then rubs at his forehead.

"What's wrong?" I ask him.

"You weren't supposed to see that. Not yet." He puts his hand on his thigh, then looks around the storage room. It feels colder than ever. "Well, I always knew this would happen. Just never thought it would be so soon. We need to have a talk."

I'd always heard about "the talk" growing up, and my face got hot as I anticipated the awkward re-telling of things I've known for a while now, thanks to a bored afternoon hanging out with my friends and the internet.

Instead of talking about the birds and the bees, my dad shows me the photo of the face. This time the wonder is gone, and I feel only terror. Were the eyes such a piercing green before?

"This is Grampa."

"Is it... like... Halloween? A mask?"

"A mask?" Dad says. "Yeah, in a way." He rubs at his forehead again. "Did your mom and I ever tell you how Gramma died?"

I think back to every conversation we've had about her, which isn't many. "No. Just that she died when I was a baby."

"This is all going to be very confusing for you. Maybe scary. I just want you to know that you're completely normal, okay? Everything I'm about to tell you is normal."

"Dad, what do you mean?"

"Your grandmother was eaten."

I stare at him for a second. Then I realize he has nothing else to say. "Eaten?"

He nods. "By Grampa."

I'm confused. I look back down at the photograph. The long, wavy hair, the facial structure, as twisted as it looks… that *is* Grampa. "I don't understand."

"It's genetic," Dad says. "Like baldness, or diabetes. It runs in the family, you know?"

"What does?"

"The *hunger*."

As he says it, my stomach growls. But I mean, I've been in the storage room for hours, working on cleaning. Of course I'm hungry.

"We're careful about it," Dad continues. "Grampa… he just slipped up. He waited too long to eat. And Gramma was the only one around. I… haven't really ever forgiven him. But I can't exactly blame him, either."

A few cold, drawn-out seconds pass, and then I bust out laughing. "Okay. Very funny, Dad. Good one."

Dad only shakes his head, then he twists it hard to the right to crack his neck. "I thought you were too young for it. But I guess the sooner you find out, the safer you'll be." Dad stands up. He rubs around at his forehead, lifts away at the hair forming the earliest shape of a widow's peak, and reveals a small, metal clasp. Dad takes it in his hands, and with a *clack-clack-clack* that echoes through the storage room, slowly unzips his face.

As the metal teeth let go of each other, two flaps of skin fall away to either side of his face. Below is blood red tissue, not quite muscle but not quite bone, and the zipper becomes visibly tighter as he gets toward this mouth. Dad pushes against one side of his jaw with his free hand, and with a *pop!* the zipper slides the rest of the way down, revealing a mouth easily twice as wide as any human's should be. I can see what used to be his teeth still there, but filling in all that extra space are yellowish, razor-sharp spires of bone.

As he sees my confusion, Dad grips one of his front teeth between his fingers and pulls so hard, he has to close his eyes—piercing green now—and then yanks out his tooth. I cover my eyes and wince, and a few seconds later, I look to see the same jagged bone in place of what was once a normal tooth. Dad is holding said tooth in his fingers.

"They're fake. Yours are too, you know. Eventually we'll have to get them re-sized. Probably pretty soon, here." Dad's voice is different now, and why not? He has twice as many teeth, his lips—if you can call them that—are a completely different shape. I'm surprised he can talk at all.

"Dad, you're scaring me."

Dad hugs me, which is the last thing I want, but as he presses my head into his chest, I feel comforted, I feel warm. He is, after all, my dad.

"It's okay. It'll be okay."

A thought slowly dawns on me. I had a cat who ran away two years ago. "Dad, remember Jester?"

Dad tousles my hair. I'm afraid to look up. I feel him moving around, and then I hear that same *clack-clack-clack*. I wince, but when I find the courage to look up, my dad looks the same as he ever did. He's tucking the last metal bit, the clasp, back under a fold of skin right at his hairline.

"Don't be silly," Dad says. "I would never eat your cat. Let's get the last of this stuff out to the car."

We carry the last few boxes and bags we've prepared outside. Dad slams the trunk, then looks off toward the last fifth of the sun still visible above the horizon. The chilly Spring wind dies down, and I swear I hear his stomach growl. "Thanks for helping me out today, champ," he says. "What say after we drop this stuff off, I take you out for dinner?"

Out in the Woods
(Continued from page 166 X2-1-2)

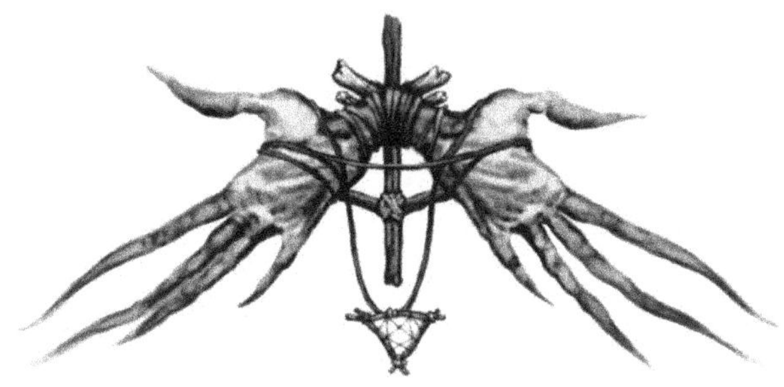

"We'll get help," Jessie said.

"Yeah," Mark replied. With heavy hearts, Jessie, Mark, Steph, and Andy pressed on, snaking their way through the trees. Now and then the air grew thick with fog, their ears filled with haze, but soon the trees opened up on the road.

"This way," Steph said. They ran down the road, pushing themselves to their limits, until the flashlight beam bounced off of a reflector.

"My car!" Mark said. He unlocked it and the four of them got inside.

Their phones didn't work, and Jessie expected the same of the car. Mark turned the key, and the engine came to life. He pulled a U-turn and stepped on the gas, pushing the car toward town.

"Keep checking your phones," Jessie said. "We have to find help."

The trees thinned and gave way to small mom-and-pop shops at the edge of town, all of them darkened, unwelcoming.

"The police station is left up here," Andy said. Mark turned on his blinker and came to a red light.

"Come on," Steph said.

"It's not going to change," Jessie said. "What if that... thing out in the woods, it's like it froze time."

"This is insane," Mark said. He pressed through the red light, then came to a screeching halt. Ahead, the street was filled with fog, and the bony woman stood in the road, her root-like legs pushing right through the asphalt.

A loud but calm, earthy voice filled everyone's ears.

Children, come.

"She's... calling," Andy said. He unbuckled his seatbelt.

"Andy, what are you doing?" Jessie said, but she realized she was reaching for her own. Andy had already opened his door.

Come to Mother.

"Fuck that!" Mark shouted. He put on his child locks and floored the gas. Andy shook his head, buckled himself back up, and braced for impact. Jessie took Steph's hand in one hand and clutched the overhead handle with the other.

Through the windshield, fog filled the world. The static haze was deafening. Then, in an instant, it was all gone: the fog, the static, the bony woman. Mark slowed to a stop and the teens looked around, but even the cracks in the pavement were gone.

"Is... is she gone?" Andy asked.

Jessie took out her phone and unlocked it. The clock at the top of her screen read 1:47. She called Melissa, but the call went straight to voicemail. Mark tried John, but it went the same. He shifted gears and continued toward the police station.

Nobody in town believed their story. Melissa and John were never found, and the four of them were suspects in their disappearance, but with no signs of foul play, they were never charged. That didn't matter to any of their classmates, neighbors, even parents; nobody looked at them the same.

With time they grew apart, moving to different towns. On the rare occasions any of them spoke to each other, it was never about the events in the woods.

Jessie made a conscious effort to avoid televisions, radios, and, when she could, cell phones. She couldn't handle the sound of static, and she had panic attacks whenever she saw fog. She stuck to an analog watch, dreading the day the second hand would cease to move, the fog would roll in, and the creature from the woods would call out to her again.

Crypto Bizarro

It Came from Outer Space
by
Josh Leichliter

Logan Gimble worked overnight at the local grocery store, stocking shelves and doing other odd jobs. Bethel was a small town, so the night crew consisted of just him and the night manager, Mandi Morsi. Everyone loved Logan; he was a kind-hearted old prankster that always found new ways to entertain (or annoy) the people of Bethel.

It was around 3 A.M. when Logan went outside to break down boxes for recycling. The alley behind the store was dark; a single light shone from above the grocery store's back door. Logan was only a few boxes in when he noticed a figure lurking just beyond the halo of light from above the door. Logan's heart lurched into his throat, but he acted cool, like he hadn't seen anything.

He kept working, keeping one wary eye on the black apparition and one on his task. He thought it might be one of the drunks stumbling home from Mae's Tavern, which was only half a block away. Perhaps Billy Martin, or Hans Krogh, two of the most notorious local scumbags. Whoever it was must've climbed the twelve-foot fence that surrounded the property. Logan gripped his boxcutter tightly, ready to defend himself if necessary.

The shadowy figure hadn't moved an inch in the fifteen minutes since he first noticed it. Logan began to suspect a prank. It was probably just a discarded mannequin from the used clothing store across the street. As he finished with the boxes, Logan's curiosity got the better of him, and he decided to have a closer look. He took a few steps toward the figure, creeped out by the way it just stood there in the dark, perfectly still, watching him. "Hey man, joke's up. Get outta here, this is private property." His crackling voice betrayed his bravado. "That you Hans? Billy? Go home, ya drunk, or I'm gonna call the sheriff!"

No response.

"Hey!" Logan tried one final time. He walked slowly closer, and his eyes focused to reveal some unworldly, twisted thing.

Suddenly the figure jerked forward, stepping partially into the light. Logan gasped and jumped backward, fumbling his boxcutter off into the darkness. The figure was human-like, but its anatomy was all wrong. Overly long arms dangled at its sides as blackened fingertips scraped the ground. Wrinkled folds of flesh creased every joint, its skin pale, almost translucent. Black, bulbous eyes fixated on him. It looked almost... alien. It lurched forward awkwardly, like it was just learning how to walk.

Logan decided to make good on his threat to call the sheriff and lunged for the door, just as it slammed shut. "What the hell? Mandi! Mandi let me in!" He banged violently on the door. "Mandi, let me in God dammit!" The door didn't budge.

Logan turned around slowly, dread building with the cold realization that there was nowhere to run. He was defenseless, and the thing was only yards away, its arms now stretched forward like a zombie eager for flesh. Its heavy breathing was the only sound in the alley. Logan's heart pounded so hard he thought it might burst.

Logan first saw stars, then felt a searing pain shoot up his arm and into his chest. His world faded to black as he slumped to ground.

The quiet night erupted with laughter. Despite being a terrible human being, Hans Krogh was also a skilled artist. He took off the alien mask he had fashioned and stared down at Logan. Mandi, his wife, unlocked the back door and stepped out, giggling. They had gotten Logan good this time: A plan they hatched in retaliation for a prank he had pulled two weeks before.

"Get up old man, we were just messin' with ya," Hans said. "Logan? Logan, get up! Shit, is he ok?"

Mandi leaned in to feel for a pulse. "No," she replied with a quivering voice.

Forever and After
by
David J. Lovato

We were so young when we fell in love,
And bought a house on a hill by the sea
So unaware that the angels and demons
Looked on at us with eyes full of envy.

I recall how we danced and we laughed
Curled up late nights by the fireplace
And all of the stupid old jokes I would tell
Managed to put a smile on your face.

But the creatures above, they wiped out our love
Sent you sickness that stifled your laughter
And gave me nothing but health so that I
Would have to suffer forever and after.

But I found a safe place to stash you away,
And the angels and demons can't stop it
I mixed up some potions and conjured up spells
And stored them and you in the closet.

I don't even care that your nails and your hair
Have grown out and onto the floor
I still love you, I always will love you
Forever and after some more.

I don't mind whether your skin's dried like leather,
It's still soft as silk in my hands
Or how when I rub at the nape of your neck
You shed flakes like hourglass sands.

And if you should lose a finger or two,
I don't mind at all, my dear love
Because in my arms you will always be safe
From the angels and demons above.

I'll spend many hours out picking flowers
And adorn you to cover that smell
You know I will bring you whatever you need
To make sure you always feel well.

I'll cut you some slack as your eyeballs roll back
And your nose caves into your head,
And your stomach puffs up and your insides come out
I'll still love you until I am dead.

And although your face has withered away
I'll always remember your smile
While your skin pulls away from your teeth and you grin
Because I'll sleep beside you awhile.

Corpse in the Closet
by
Josh Leichliter

Slick, red and wet, its voice frail and grim
it hung in the closet, a thing with no skin
It whispered in secrets, babbled in schemes
corrupted and dire draconian themes

A hymn of black ash, it beckoned and sung
It pleaded for bedlam and hell to be done
I could bear it no longer, I'd settle the score
I sealed off the hallway and bricked up the door

I still hear the whimpers, the demonic screams
thumping and wailing consumes every dream
It poisons my mind with visions of gore
It rakes at my soul as it bangs on that door

It hangs there, upstairs, in the closet, you see?
The corpse with no skin is devouring me

81

A Night at the Old Train Station
by
David J. Lovato

"Working late again, Manabe?"

Takumi Manabe looked up from the papers before him. The light was gone from the windows, and most of the rest of the cubicles were empty. He glanced at his computer monitor. It was almost eight o'clock.

"I guess so," Manabe said.

Kato chuckled. "Don't you take the old train home? Aren't you afraid of being out at that station after dark?"

Manabe leaned back in his chair and rubbed his eyes. He had a migraine, and had only just noticed it. "Why would I be afraid of that?"

Kato raised an eyebrow. "You haven't heard the legends?"

"What legends?"

Kato stepped the rest of the way into Manabe's cubicle. "I can't believe you've been taking that old train—forever, and you haven't heard about the Teke-Teke."

"I guess I don't pay much attention to children's stories."

"It's not a children's story," Kato said. "Twenty years ago, a girl got run over by the train."

Manabe rolled his eyes. Maybe he wouldn't be staying so late if his coworkers didn't bother him with silly fables. Oh, who was he kidding? He'd become a workaholic ever since Umeko had broken up with him. It kept his mind off of things. "That's tragic."

"It cut her completely in half!" Kato said. He flinched, looked around, and then continued, more quietly. "They say she now haunts the old train station at nights. Her spirit is restless; she's jealous of the life she never got to live, so when she finds you, she tears you in half, just like her."

"It's just an old legend," Manabe said. "I'm sure we'd notice if there were halves of people lying around the train station."

Kato shook his head. "She must do something with the bodies. Nobody has ever found one, but a lot of people have gone missing around that station over the years. That's why they built the new rail system, Manabe. But they had to leave the old one open because they couldn't run the mono out to some of the rural areas."

Manabe realized he had put his pencil down; he'd apparently become engrossed in the story. Now he sighed. "Come on, Kato, think for a second. If she cuts her victims in half and nobody finds them, how would anyone know that's what happened to those missing people?"

Kato gave Manabe a funny look, something he'd never seen on him before. "Same way any legends pass along, Manabe. She *doesn't* get everyone. Sometimes people get away. My uncle swears he saw her before."

"If he's anything like you, he's full of it."

"He's not like me. He's serious, Manabe. I'd bet everything I have on him telling the truth. The old man doesn't mess around."

Manabe shrugged. "Everyone has a little fun from time to time."

"He didn't seem like he was having fun. The way he looked when he told me... and he only told me because I mentioned I was going out to that station one day. The color just left him, Manabe. And he described her like he was seeing her right then and there. Said he was out at the old station after a night of drinking—"

"There's your problem right there."

"He doesn't even drink that much. But he and an old war buddy of his went out on the town, and he didn't want to drive, so they went out to the station. He said this half of a girl came at them. He wanted to run, but his buddy wanted *Msaudju sm pfu mzxdw zy wunw mpnim. Mpnpsj sm pfu mzxdw zy ofnpurui vsaauw pfuc.* to fight. He was drunk, see. But this girl, she moved so fast—made this *tek tek* sound the whole way, dragging her insides along the ground. And she grabbed my uncle's buddy. My uncle just ran then. Said he looked back once and saw the girl had torn his friend in half, like it was nothing. He just kept running. When he came back with the police, there was nothing there. No girl, no sign of his friend, no blood, nothing. But nobody ever saw him again."

Manabe thought for a while. "I won't say your uncle didn't see something. But that's just not possible, Kato. It's just a story meant to scare people."

"Sure," Kato said. All of the playfulness had left him, he seemed drained, almost sad. "You're probably right, Manabe."

Manabe went back to his work, but he couldn't help feeling a little shaken.

<hr>

It only took a few minutes of work for Manabe to forget all about the conversation he'd had with Kato, but that night, as he stood alone at the old train station, it was all he could think about.

A warm breeze stirred, and that calmed him. The trees shook gently, the air smelled of sakura flowers. Most of the mono stations were indoors, but the old trains still had the classic outdoor platforms, with only a little canopy to block the rain. The only building was a small booth for a guard to stand in, but it had been unmanned for a long time, now.

Manabe heard the sound of footsteps on gravel. He looked up the sidewalk leading onto the train platform, but couldn't see much beyond the glow of the nearest streetlight. Slowly a shape took form, then an old man appeared beneath the light, dressed in a suit and tie and carrying a briefcase. Slowly, he made his way onto the platform. Manabe waved, but the man only squinted at him, then shut his eyes.

As unfriendly as he was, at least Manabe wasn't alone anymore.

A few quiet moments went by, and then the gentle breeze was replaced by the sound of two people talking. It was low at first, but now and then a discernible word or laugh broke out. A young man and young woman, both clearly tipsy, approached the train platform. Manabe felt better than ever. He smiled at the thought of Kato's dumb story spooking him.

"Hey man, got a smoke?"

Manabe turned, but the young man wasn't talking to him. The old man opened his eyes just enough to glare at the young man, then closed them again. The young guy turned to his girlfriend.

"What's that guy's deal?" He jerked his thumb as though he wasn't aware that, from about two feet away, the old man could still hear them talking about him.

The young woman giggled. "Probably disapproves."

"What about you?"

"I don't smoke," Manabe said. "Sorry."

The young man looked wounded. Then he shrugged. "Bummer."

The couple resumed their giggling and talking, somewhat quieter now. The old man was silent as ever. Over it all, a low, repetitive sound broke in, quietly at first, but rapidly growing louder.

"That'll be the train," Manabe said. It was still pretty far off. The young couple stopped talking to listen.

Tek tek tek tek tek tek tek.

The young couple just went back to talking, but Manabe's heart leapt into his throat. He wiped his forehead, then forced a smile. How foolish of him; that was just the train chugging along the tracks.

The sound got closer, but not much louder. *Tek tek tek tek tek tek.* Four sets of eyes followed it from the darkness and along the tracks, but there was no train. The sound slowed and came to a halt right in front of the platform.

Up hopped the torso of a young girl. Her hair was mangy and thin, her skin barely clung to her bones, and when she landed on the palms of her hands, the tattered remains of her insides smacked against the wood of the train platform: *Tek tek tek.*

The young couple screamed. The old man gasped. Manabe stood, mouth agape, his brain still trying to come up with some way this must not be real. Then his mouth closed almost into a smile: It had to be a puppet. Kato was playing one of his idiotic pranks.

"Kato!" Manabe shouted.

"You... know this girl?" the tipsy man asked.

Tek tek tek tek tek tek tek tek. The half-girl sprinted across the platform, walking on her hands faster than Manabe had ever seen a human run. Before he could react, she was past him, and by the time he had turned to follow where she went, the tipsy girl was screeching in terror. The creature was on her boyfriend's shoulders, biting into his neck with rows of pointed teeth.

"This girl's insane! Get her off me!"

It was the old man who stepped forward, swinging his briefcase with both hands. It connected with the girl's scraggly head, and she went somersaulting through the air, trailing droplets of blood. She landed on her hands, a grin plastered across her face.

The tipsy man covered the wound with both hands. "You bit me!"

The girl balanced herself on one limb. With the other she folded her fingers into some kind of pose Manabe didn't recognize. Then she flattened them out, stretched her hand all the way to her left, and sliced it through the air as quick as she could.

The tipsy man split in half. Blood spewed out as though it had been under pressure. His legs stumbled forward, and his top half fell backward onto the platform with a dull splat.

The old man vomited. The tipsy woman screamed. The little girl, meanwhile, turned her eyes to her victim's girlfriend, then started to form that same symbol with her fingers.

Manabe rushed forward. His limbs acted on their own; he wanted to run away, but instead he headed straight for the quickly sobering young woman. He dove forward, shoving her as hard as he could, just as the little girl sliced through the air again. Something like a gust of wind pushed at Manabe's back, and he landed hard on his hands and knees, rolling in time to see a small section of his shirt fluttering to the ground.

Manabe took a second to orient himself. The young woman was sprinting down the sidewalk, there was no sign of the old man except for the vomit he'd left, and the half of a little girl was sitting up on her hands, grinning at Manabe.

"What do you want?" Manabe shouted. The smile disappeared from the creature's face, her eyes widened. Then she grinned even wider.

"What's my name?"

Her voice was inhuman, weak, sounding almost like it was underwater.

"W-what?" Manabe said.

"You have... what I never will!" She lifted a hand and her fingers started to curl.

Manabe grabbed a nearby rock and tossed it as hard as he could, smacking the girl's standing hand out from under her. She tumbled to the platform, and Manabe wasted no time. He rushed forward and kicked her as hard as he could; her frail body rolled across the platform and off of it, onto the railroad tracks.

Manabe ran for the streetlights and the sidewalk beyond them, then he felt something grab him and pull. He hit his head and his side on something, winced, and then tried to shout, but the old man put his hand over Manabe's mouth.

"Shhh," he said. He seemed calm, almost more annoyed than afraid. Quietly, he shut the door of the little guard booth.

"She'll find us in here," Manabe said.

"We just have to wait," the old man replied.

"For what?"

The old man raised an eyebrow. "The train," he said, like it was obvious. But then, it almost was; surely the creature would be frightened off by the very thing that had killed her—

Manabe had a thought. He reached into his pocket and pulled out his cell phone.

Fear lit up the old man's face. "You idiot, if you call the police, she'll hear you talking! There's no way they'll get here in time!"

"Shhh," Manabe replied. He showed the old man his screen, open to an internet browser.

Manabe opened up a search engine and typed *little girl killed train chiisagata district*. The reception out here wasn't the best, and Manabe watched as a tiny blue bar crept from one side of his phone's screen toward the other.

Tek tek.

Slowly, quietly, Manabe slid up the wall of the guard booth, just enough to peek through the grimy window. He could barely see, but the creature was definitely out there, wandering around on her hands, *tek tek tek*-ing as she went, looking for her prey. *Tek tek tek.* She walked along the platform, away from the guard booth, out of sight.

Manabe sighed, let himself relax, and then the girl slammed into the window before him. With a shout, Manabe jumped backward, almost into the old man's lap, dropping his phone in the process. The old man clutched Manabe's arm, both of them stared out the little window at the creature propped up on her hands on the wood just beyond the glass. Manabe's gut sank; he had a feeling he was about to find out what Teke-Teke did with all those halves of bodies.

The girl balanced herself on one hand, then pounded the other against the glass. It made several dull thuds, then she formed her hand sign and sliced at the air. The glass window exploded, raining bits and pebbles onto Manabe and the old man. Manabe looked down to cover himself, then noticed his phone had finally loaded the page.

Manabe stood up. "Miki Ishikawa!"

The creature in the window lowered her hand and stood still. Her grin was gone, her eyes drooped.

"Your name, it's Miki Ishikawa. We haven't forgotten you, see?" Manabe turned his phone so the Teke-Teke could see the website article about her tragedy.

A horn blared out. Light poured onto the train platform, along with the increasingly loud clattering of train wheels, which soon became a screech as the train pulled up to the platform. When the light passed the guard booth, the Teke-Teke was gone.

Manabe looked around. Broken glass littered the station, the old man was standing up and dusting himself off, and there was no sign of any blood or either half of the tipsy man. There was only the warm breeze and the smell of sakura flowers wafting in the air.

When he got home that night, Manabe called Umeko, just to hear her voice. He let her know he was sorry things didn't work out, and that he wished her well. He stopped working late nights. Not out of fear of seeing the Teke-Teke again, but because he still had too much to live for.

Out in the Woods
(Continued from page 51 X1-2)

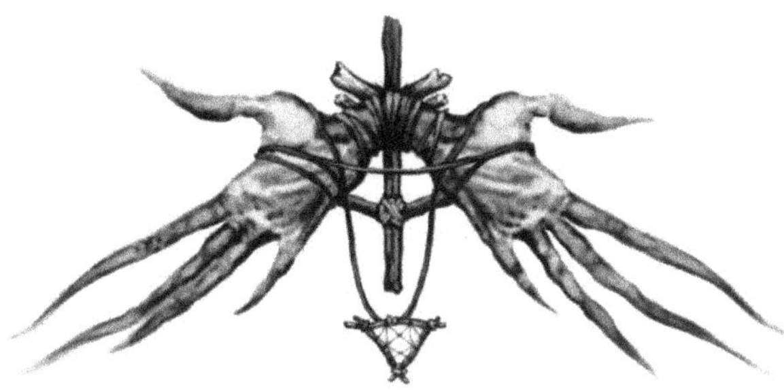

Jessie left her sleeping bag and crawled a few feet to where Melissa lay. "Hey," she said. Melissa didn't move. Jessie nudged her shoulder. "Melissa, wake up."

"What?"

"My phone's not working. Look."

Melissa squinted from the light, then rolled over, away from Jessie. "Turn it off and back on."

"It's not working, Melissa. And something's wrong. I think there's an animal or something nearby."

"Jessie, quit it. You're starting to freak me out."

"Listen."

Neither of the girls said anything. The woods were still and silent as a tomb.

"Jessie, put some headphones in and go back to sleep."

Jessie crawled back into her sleeping bag, but sleep was the furthest thing from her mind. Time crawled by, her heart beat faster and faster. She looked into the darkness again, hoping to see someone else awake, but saw only the trees. Jessie looked at her phone: 1:44. Wrong. She looked up again, waited for her eyes to re-adjust to the darkness, then noticed someone standing up on their sleeping bag.

"Steph," Jessie whispered. "You okay?"

Steph was silent for a second, then replied, "She's calling."

"What? Who? Is your phone working?"

Steph lifted a hand and pointed beyond the clearing, into the trees. Jessie squinted, and then she saw it, too.

Standing tall, in the space between the trees, only distinguishable from them because it was so thin, was what looked like the silhouette of a woman. Her head was round, probably bald, and her skin was thin and ridged like tree bark. She had to be at least eight feet tall.

The woman spread her arms, as if to offer a hug, and Steph took a few steps toward her.

"Steph, what are you doing?"

"She's calling," Steph said without looking back.

Jessie shot to her feet. "Who are you? What do you want?"

The others started to stir. Steph walked faster.

"Stop!" Jessie shouted. She started toward Steph, but she was already within reach of the gaunt woman. Jessie stopped as a mass of darkness protruded from the woman—long vine-like appendages burst from her back, or maybe her front, she couldn't tell. They writhed and wiggled in the darkness, impossible limbs, like tentacles. A second later they lashed forward, grabbing at Steph and tearing her apart like wet paper, splashing the trees and grass with blood. The embers of the fire sizzled as a few drops pattered against them, and Jessie covered her eyes from a stream of blood flung her way.

When she lowered her arm, the bony woman was gone, and Steph was gone, except for the blood. Mark was screaming, running to where she had been, but John and Andy grabbed him. He tried to tear free from them. Melissa was crying, jerking her head now and then as if she'd heard something.

John let go of Mark and took out his phone. Mark broke free from Andy and rushed to the edge of the clearing, where bits and pieces of his sister still lay all over the ground and hung from the branches.

Andy came straight to Jessie and hugged her tight. She hugged him back.

"My phone isn't working," John said.

"Same here," Jessie replied.

Nobody could get past their lock screen, and everyone's phone was stuck at the same time, except for Melissa's; hers was stuck at 1:45.

"So... what happens now?" Andy asked.

"We find the bitch," Mark replied. He was still crouched at the edge of the clearing, but he stood up and rushed over to the others. "We find her and we fuck her up."

The others looked at each other. "Mark," Jessie said. "Did you not see what... that thing, it's not human."

"It was dark," Mark said.

"Look around," John said. "I'm not trying to be mean, but look. A person couldn't do that."

"We need to get out of the woods," Andy said. "That thing might as well be camouflaged."

"We have to get help," Melissa said. "We need to get to the road, get to our cars."

John kneeled down and unzipped his bag. He pulled two flashlights out. "These should help."

"How do we get back?" Mark asked. "No phones means no GPS."

"Fuck," Andy said.

"We came from that way, right?" Jessie asked. She pointed. "We can walk back that way. In as straight a line as we can. Might not end up taking the shortest route, but we should hit the road at some point."

"I don't remember," Melissa said. "Are you sure?"

Jessie looked again, but there were no visual bearings, only trees. Did one move? She yanked a flashlight from John and turned it on, pointing it in that direction, but saw only the closest trees to the flashlight's warm glow.

"We could end up going deeper into the woods," Mark said.

"No, it's that way," Jessie said. "Look, the log we've been sitting on. I remember Melissa came into the clearing and sat straight on it. It was parallel to the way we came, see?"

"But from which end?"

Jessie looked one way, then the other, then back again. This time, at the very edge of the flashlight's glow, she saw white, and movement.

"Guys..." Jessie said.

"It was that way," Mark said. "Ninety percent sure."

"That way is farther from the log," Melissa said. "I don't think I walked that—"

"Guys!" Jessie shouted.

They turned to where the light was pointed, and nobody moved. The bony woman stood, barely visible, still as a statue.

"This has to be a prank," Melissa said.

Mark pointed to the mess in the other direction. Most of the group turned to look. "Does that look like a fucking prank?"

"There's such a thing as fake blood—"

"Steph wouldn't do that!"

Jessie kept her eyes fixed on the bony woman. She came closer; she didn't walk, but the skin of her legs grew up from the ground ahead of her and back into it behind, like she was growing along the ground. As she came, fog thickened into existence, and a hazy sound invaded Jessie's ears.

"Oh God, she's getting closer!" Jessie shouted. She turned and ran, grabbing Andy's arm as she passed, and when he followed, the others did as well.

"This is the wrong way!" Andy said.

"Not right now it's not!" Jessie replied. She found the bigger gaps between the trees, turned to her right, went a few yards out that way, then turned again, this time skirting their campsite and, she hoped, the gaunt creature.

Jessie wasn't sure how long she ran before looking back, but when she did, she saw only Andy and Mark. She stopped.

"Where are the others?"

Mark turned around, then back to her. "They were behind me before."

"How long ago?"

"I don't know."

"We have to go back," Andy said.

"Toward that thing?" Mark looked over his shoulder, then back again. "You sure?"

To go back for the others, turn to page X1-4 (98).
To keep going, turn to page X1-5 (125).

Crypto Bizarro

93

The Girl Without a Mask
by
Aerys Bates-Leichliter

The boy in red moved toward the black building. It was that time of year again; the Cleansers were expecting each and every resident to be searched and cleansed of sin. The boy in red had gone before with his parents, but that was long ago. His parents had since broken the rules and been thrown to the Howlers.

The boy took shaky breaths as he entered the dark building. There, three men greeted him.

"What is your name?" asked a man dressed in black and red, with a smile plastered on his white mask.

Ryo straightened his back. "Tamaki, Ryo, age 15."

"Which Region?" asked another man, who was wearing little clothing, with a sad expression indented in his mask.

"Black Smile" Ryo said, pointing to the smile on his mask.

"Walk this way" said a third man, covered head to toe in blue and orange cloth.

They guided him to a white room with a Cleanser standing near the back. "Now please, remove your clothing, this includes your mask," the Cleanser said.

Ryo stripped, finishing with the mask. He hadn't felt air on his face in a long time.

The men gathered his clothes and left. The Cleanser emerged from around a dark, seemingly endless pool that extended beyond his view. Being particularly adept, only females are allowed the role of Cleanser. This one's face was hidden behind a painted mask that blended into her sallow skin. Her hands were stained with a black substance, her curvy body wrapped in a soaking white kimono. Her arms were contorted, and her legs thin and pale.

"My dear, hopeless child." Her voice was gravelly and harsh. Slowly, she limped over to Ryo. The Cleanser wrapped her disfigured arms tightly around his chest. "What is it... that you hide?" She slid a bony black hand into his mouth, prying open his jaw. Ryo remained silent, he did not want to end up like his parents. "Show me... your secrets." She reached into Ryo's throat, scratching the insides of his chest with her sharp fingernails. A bead of sweat dripped from his head. "Almost there." She chuckled a bit, then reached farther into his body. "Ah! There." She grabbed the hot, flaming ball that was his soul and unceremoniously wrenched it out.

The ball was a dull pink color. "I see... I remember this feeling... oh, so long ago... but I no longer know what love is." Her voice trailed off as she embraced the warmth that was emanating from Ryo's exposed soul.

Ryo closed his eyes and gritted his teeth. The fact that his soul was so easily read bothered him. "What a beautiful young girl. I remember my young years." The Cleanser wrapped her claw-like hands around the glowing orb. "Oh, this is... your partner? Ah, what a shame. She could do so much better." She snorted. Ryo snarled at her remark. "So that's what you were trying to hide, hmmm?" She placed a finger on Ryo's eye. "This is a punishable crime. You know that, right?" She glanced at Ryo. "She broke her mask... and you were trying to hide her from the nation, weren't you?" The Cleanser sneered. Ryo stiffened and remained silent.

"What a pitiful sin. Almost feel bad for you, but as you know, she will have to be thrown to the Howlers. As for you..." The Cleanser grabbed Ryo's jaw and forced it open. She placed his soul back into his mouth, then gently pressed up on his chin. His eyes widened in fear.

"Don't! Please... It was my fault she broke her mask." Ryo clenched his fists in anger. "I was trying to help her! She was having the dream again. She was crying... I did everything I could to wake her!" Ryo was shaking. "She grabbed me, tried to choke me, I... I pushed her. She fell and her mask shattered. She woke up, she was so scared... I tried to fix the mask, but I couldn't..." Sweat trickled from his brow, his voice shaking. "Just please... please don't throw her to the Howlers! Take me instead!" Overcome with emotion, Ryo lowered his head and quietly sobbed.

"Hmmm, perhaps that could be arranged." Ryo gasped in disbelief as the Cleanser circled around him. "But would you really do that? Risk your life for the one you love?" She smirked. "That would be quite a show..." She limped to the door and opened it. The Cleanser exchanged brief whispers with a new figure dressed in black, his mask golden. She shut the door quietly and turned to face Ryo. "Listen boy, here's the deal: we will throw *you* to the Howlers instead, *but* you must kill the Alpha. If you succeed, we will take you to your friend, and replace her mask. If you do not... we will throw your cherished one in with you, and you will both perish." She chuckled as she stroked Ryo's unkempt black hair. "Deal?" She raised her long, bony hand toward Ryo.

"Deal." He shook her hand, attempting to mask his fear. The Cleanser chuckled. "Good luck, boy. You'll need it."

The Cleanser shoved Ryo into the pool of dark, brackish water. He sank slowly, gasping. His lungs filled with the putrid substance, until his vision blurred and the darkness took him.

Ryo awoke on a plateau of mossy black rocks. The air was polluted and rotten, and the scent of death lingered all around him. His clothes were different now, and his mask had been replaced. This new mask was heavy, uncomfortable.

His neck hurt, and his head bobbed with the unfamiliar weight. He wondered what it looked like, but dared not take it off to see.

When his eyes adjusted to the dark, Ryo spied black, jagged rocks around him, scattered with bones, broken masks, and decaying flesh. He rose to his feet and slowly crept forward into the darkness, carefully avoiding the fragile bones. He heard the clicking footsteps of the Howlers following him, though he could not see them. They were toying with him, he assumed, assessing their new prey.

Distant screams echoed throughout the vast, black valley. Were those victims, or the Howlers themselves? Ryo had never been so afraid. The clicking drew nearer as he quickened his pace. His heart began to pound as they grew louder, now directly behind him.

A shrill, distorted voice rang out in the dark: "Turn around."

Ryo's heart stuttered as he stopped, and slowly turned. He could never have imagined the horror that stood before him now. He knew that this was the Alpha.

Steeling himself, he clenched his fists and took a deep breath. "For a new mask!" he declared proudly, and lunged.

Out in the Woods
(Continued from page 92 X1-4)

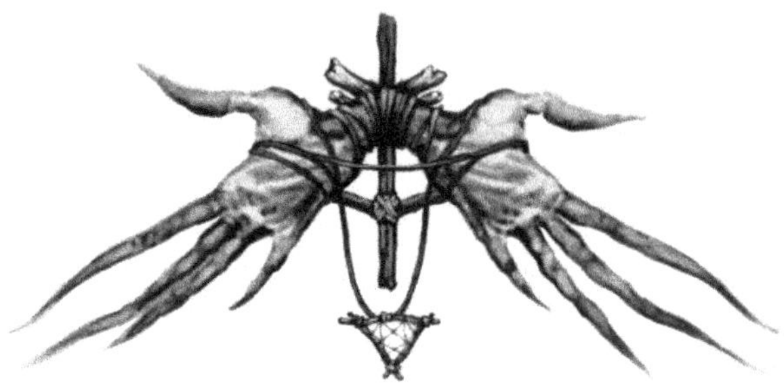

"We can't leave them behind," Jessie said.

"Turn off the flashlight for a second," Mark said. "Maybe we'll see theirs out there."

Jessie turned off her flashlight. For a second she could see absolutely nothing, and she had to fight the urge to turn the light back on. Slowly, her eyes adjusted to the dark, and then she saw something: A flicker of light, somewhat back the way they'd come, but off to the side.

"There," she said. She started toward the light.

"Wait," Andy said. He looked around at the ground, picked up a rock, and scratched an arrow into a nearby tree.

The trio headed toward their friends, shouting and waving their arms. A few seconds later, Melissa and John appeared out of the woods. Melissa threw her arms around Jessie.

"We were so scared. We got lost."

"It's okay now," Jessie said. "This way, we're almost there."

She turned her flashlight on and turned back toward the tree with the arrow in it. She pointed the light at a few of the trees, and found the arrow. She took a step toward it, but Andy grabbed her hand. The others weren't moving. Jessie looked more closely, and again saw the faint silhouette at the edge of the light.

"We need to go around," Jessie said.

"She's calling," Andy replied. He let go of Jessie's hand and took a step forward.

"Andy!"

Andy stopped, but didn't turn. He took another step forward, more slowly this time.

"Andy, don't walk toward it!"

Jessie heard the sound in her mind grow louder, and the creature was closer, ahead of the arrow tree now. She could swear her vision was covered by a layer of fog as a booming but calm voice filled her ears, louder than her own thoughts.

Come to me, child.

"No!" Jessie shouted.

John took a step toward the bony woman.

Don't you understand? I'm in control of everything.

"She's calling," Melissa said.

"Fight it!" Jessie replied.

More white noise, more fog, and the creature came closer, but only by a few inches.

"We can push her back!" Jessie said. She took Andy's hand in one of hers, and Melissa's in the other. The entire group held hands and stood together.

The creature moved, but this time farther away.

Come to me, children. Where you belong.

"Never!"

A second passed. The fog was gone from Jessie's vision, and the creature was far away, at the edge of the light, her pale body and outstretched hands barely visible. She laughed, so softly, quiet now.

But I need you.

Another second passed, and she was gone.

The teens stood still a moment, listening, but there was no fog, no white noise, just the glow of their flashlights focused on a tree pointing them out of the woods.

"Is it gone?" John asked.

Jessie had an idea. She was careful not to move the flashlight as she reached into her pocket and took out her phone. A smile spread across her face as she saw the time read 1:45. She swiped on the screen, and her phone unlocked.

"It's gone," Jessie said. Together, the teens headed among the trunks of the trees, which eventually stopped and became the road.

Melissa checked her GPS. "We parked over this way," she said, and the group started up the road.

"Mark," Jessie said. "I'm so sorry about your sister."

"...Yeah," Mark said. The air was thick, nobody seemed to know what to say.

Jessie took Andy's hand. She knew ahead would be sleepless nights, plagued by the things she'd seen that night, that she'd never look at fog or hear white noise the same, that their troubles were just beginning. But for now, at least, they were out of the woods.

All She Wanted
by
Sarah Carswell

She only wanted to be beautiful like them.
But she was always too plain, too gawky, too thin.
A moth overlooked midst a sea of monarch beauty.
No one cared about boring old Trudy.

But Trudy was always watching them.
Their shiny, swishing hair; their sun-kissed, rosy skin.
She wanted their beauty, and have it she would
And if she couldn't have it then nobody could

A snippet of Penelope's shiny hair
The broken red fingernail that fell off of Claire
Fragments of beauty no one would miss
Knotted around Trudy's winged wish

The petulant, pouty lips of Patrice
Carved from her lovely face as she sleeps.
Now sewn upon Trudy's twisted sneer
Waxy smile split ear to ear.

Elegant fingers once attached to Denise
Will never again tickle ivory keys
Lifeless, they hang from Trudy's hands
Like Rotting, fleshy eternity bands.

Empty eyes, shriveled and dull,
Stare lifelessly from Trudy's skull.
Liquid tempest orbs, once sapphire blue
Plucked from the sockets of Anna Lou.

The perfectly freckled and pert nose of Grace
Stitched with red ribbon across Trudy's face
Never to turn up in disdain again
The penance to pay for prideful sin.

Mounds of milky, silky flesh
Carved from Anastasia's chest
Wither on Trudy's shapeless form
Symbols of desire, self-loathing, and scorn.

The sharp, biting tongue of nasty Annette
On a delicate cord hangs from poor Trudy's neck.
Flanked by the toes of graceful Guinevere
Snapped from her feet with gardening shears

She only wanted to be beautiful like them.
But she was always too plain, too gawky, too thin.
A moth overlooked midst a sea of monarch beauty.
Now they're all part of poor twisted Trudy.

Adeli
by
Sarah Carswell

Poor Adeli
She'd never harm a fly
But the flies have to eat
So she feeds them the meat
Of the girls who make her cry

And as she serves her horde
Ben withdraws his sword
He shears off his tongue
Into the offering it's flung
His love for her lent no word

Out in the Woods
(Continued from page 26 X2)

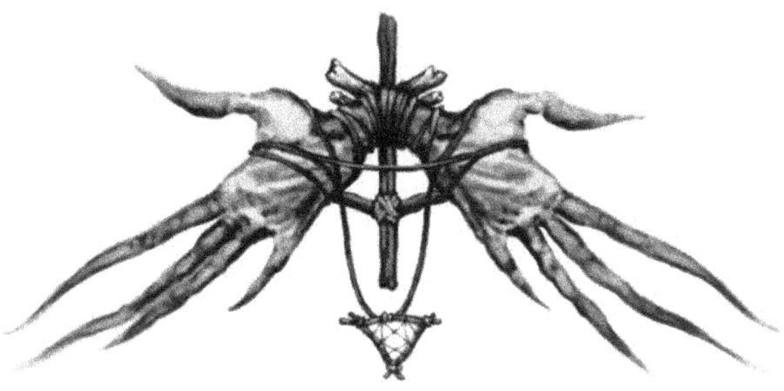

John started down the path to the right, and the others followed. The spaces between trees shrank, and to their right a small hill became a steep incline.

"Hey," Melissa said, "I think I see the fire—"

"Ack!" John screamed, and then he fell. Some leaves underfoot had slid, and the weight of his backpack pulled him the rest of the way down the incline. He tumbled over roots and fallen leaves, then came to a rest against a tree a dozen feet away.

"Shit!" Andy said. He walked quickly but carefully down the hill. Mark followed.

"You all right?" Mark asked.

"My foot," John said. "It feels broken!"

Andy crouched down for a second, then stood back up. "It's not broken. Probably not even sprained. Here." He took John's backpack, and Mark helped him up. Carefully, on their hands and feet, they crept back up the hill and onto the trail. Mark helped John walk.

"There's a little creek near the fire pit. The water gets super cold. We should soak your ankle when we find it."

Before long they reached a clearing with a ring of stones near the center. Most of the teens set to work gathering firewood and setting up chairs, while Mark helped John limp down a small slope toward a creek where he could soak his leg.

"We should probably call the whole thing off," Jessie said. "He looks pretty hurt."

"We came all the way out here," Andy said. "We just got here."

Jessie glared at him. "What if he needs a doctor?"

Andy looked at the ground. "Yeah. I guess you're right."

"I'll be fine, guys," John said.

"...How the fuck did he even hear us?" Steph said. She giggled.

"It's not like he could really walk all the way back out of the woods right now anyway," Mark said.

"Yeah, I mean, either way we're going to have to give it an hour or two. Might as well see if I end up feeling fine by then."

"You sure?" Jessie asked. John nodded.

"Jessie, look at this!" Andy said. He was carrying an abnormally large piece of firewood between his legs.

Jessie snorted and rolled her eyes. "You're an idiot."

The trees were thick out here, but the campsite was a fifteen-foot radius absent of trees, with a small fire pit near the center. Ashes and whitened coals were strewn about it, and the site was dotted with the occasional empty beer bottle.

Over by the creek, John pulled a broken flashlight from his bag. "Damn." He dug around in it a little more.

When the campsite was set up, the teens began to relax. Melissa got a fire going to combat the quickly darkening sky, and soon John joined them, sitting in a chair and resting his leg on a large tree trunk Melissa and Steph were sitting on. The teens shared conversation about their lives, about school and home and everything in between, laughing and having fun. Jessie had only met Steph and Mark a few times, and had only seen John around the halls at school, but she knew them through Andy and Melissa, and she hoped the six of them could be closer after tonight.

"Jessie," Steph said. "You should tell scary stories."

"What makes you think I know any?"

"For real, girl? You're always reading. Like, *always*."

"I veto that," Melissa said.

"You scared?" John asked.

"I'm sure I will be, if you all fall asleep before I do and I'm up all alone."

The others laughed. In the glow of the campfire, they took turns telling scary stories. It was a warm night, but Jessie had goosebumps. She rubbed her arms and looked around; the woods had the faintest haze to them, like a barely visible fog was setting in.

"Are you okay?" Andy whispered.

"Yeah. I just... kinda feel like we're being watched, or something. It's stupid."

"It's all good," Andy said. When it was his turn to tell a story, he changed tone and went for comedy, and the others followed suit. It wasn't long before John set up his sleeping bag and lay down, and eventually the stories became sparse as the teens fell asleep one by one.

Crack.

Jessie stirred. Leaves rustled, even though she felt no breeze. She sat up. The fire had burned out, and all of her friends were asleep. The fog had grown denser, and despite the lack of wind, she could hear what sounded like leaves rustling, or maybe rain, though it sounded far away.

She checked her phone. It was 1:44 A.M. She put the phone away, but then checked it again. Something was wrong; she had turned in around 1:30, and some of the others had still been awake. This didn't feel right.

Another twig cracked just outside the clearing. Jessie tried to unlock her phone, but the screen only wiggled a little and wouldn't budge. Leaves rustled a few feet away. Jessie was sweating. She decided to wake one of her friends.

To wake Andy, turn to page X2-1 (165).
To wake Melissa, turn to page X2-2 (136).

Dog's Story
by
Seth Thomas

I felt a nice breeze rush over me as I walked down the sidewalk in the quiet neighborhood. The air felt nice on my thick coat of fur. I was not alone; my friend was with me, and I walked just ahead of her. I glanced up at her face; she was always smiling at me. There was something over her ears. I'm not sure what it was, but it was strange.

Not far from our house, there was a man in his yard, and I felt an undeniable urge to bark and run at him. I couldn't overcome it, but my friend stopped me, and I began to calm down as we passed him by. The man gave us a look as he poured water from some green thing all over the flowers.

We stopped for a moment for me to go to the bathroom near a bush, and I turned to look at my friend. She seemed to be messing with some device; maybe it had something to do with the thing over her ears? I wasn't sure. She smiled down at me, and made a sound. I swung my tail back and forth, and it brushed the sidewalk.

"You ready, Skipper?" she asked in her soft human voice. My tongue was hanging from my open jaws. I was happy, ready to continue our walk. I took off, and I heard her playful pleas to slow down a bit. I did, and we were back on track.

A small black thing on the ground caught my interest, and I had to stop *U lyzh us rijs fp wkno, fīs dzi wkbp sz hklp im. Cijs hklp im vzn rp. U yppo dzi.* and investigate. My human didn't seem to mind too much. I poked it with my nose and sniffed it. When I felt it move, I freaked out and backed up a step. My big body bumped into my human's leg, and she seemed startled. I barked at the black thing, thinking it might go away. It did not. It moved a few inches over the sidewalk and then stopped.

"Come on, silly dog," my human said, laughing. I tore myself away from the black thing, then continued on.

I was growing a little tired, but I felt the need to pee again, so I stopped near a fire hydrant. When I was finished, I looked up at my friend. She looked different. She dropped the rope that was tied to the collar around my neck. I stepped over to it, sniffed it, and bumped against my human's legs.

She looked down at me, and I felt uncomfortable. Something was different about her, I could smell it. I barked at her, but she made no noise. She grunted as she began to move toward me.

What was she doing? She wasn't *my* human. Who was this human? I had to get away, and quickly, but she was standing on the rope attached to my collar. I pulled, and she took a step forward, freeing me. I got away, with the rope slapping against the sidewalk as I ran. I was terrified of this human, and didn't want anything to do with her. I wanted my old human back.

I stopped running when a big moving object came flying along the sidewalk. It hit that strange human with the strange things on her ears. The human tumbled over the top of the moving thing, and then landed in a strange shape on the grass... She kept moving after being hit. The big moving object hit a tree, one I pee on regularly. It crumpled in the front, but otherwise, it looked a lot like the thing my human would take me in when we went to the park. I missed my human.

Some other humans crowded around the crumpled object, and there were screams. The door opened, and one human tried to get out of the front, but was ripped to shreds by the other humans. One of them saw me. I bolted.

Later in the day I was running down a quiet street. There was no one on the street, no one wandering the neighborhood like there normally was. I felt a little scared all by myself, and then I heard a voice call to me. It was a human, and even though it sounded friendly, it was not my human. I turned around to bark, and instead found myself running up to the human. A man came out of a door near the woman who had called me. She knelt down as I ran to her, and she slowly reached out and patted my thick brown coat. Her hand ran down my back. I felt happy that this new human was so kind. She was not like my old human, but she was just as nice.

"What's your name, boy?" the woman asked as she took the rope off my collar. She looked at the little metal bone hanging from it, and smiled at me as she rubbed behind my ears. I wagged my tail. "Skipper! What a great name! Come on, you'll be safe from those things in here, Skipper." They let me inside; the two new humans introduced me to two smaller humans, and it was nice. I felt safe.

That night I lay in a bed of blankets in the room with the two bigger humans. I couldn't sleep right away. I worried about my human, and hoped she'd be okay. Eventually I did drift off to sleep, and I slept very well.

109

The Babysitter
by
Sarah Carswell

Plik-a-plunk.

I thought the Wilsons' flat doorbell chime sounded congested, like it had a cold. *That'll make two of us with a cold, if they don't hurry up*, I thought. The harsh winter wind whipped my hair relentlessly as I stood on the front stoop of the old home.

Just as I was about to pull out my phone to make sure I had the correct address, the front door flung open and warmth enveloped me.

"Oh, you must be Emma. I'm sorry to keep you waiting." Mrs. Wilson was an elegant lady with sad eyes. With her dark hair pulled back into a sleek twist and her long, graceful neck, I thought she resembled a professional dancer. A ballerina, perhaps.

"That's okay, Mrs. Wilson," I replied. "Yes, I'm Emma." I extended my hand. At fifteen years old, I was often told that I was mature for my age. "Thank you for letting me babysit Broderick tonight."

"Well, Emma, I've heard nothing but good things from your other clients," Mrs. Wilson replied in a reserved voice, leading me inside her home. She firmly closed the heavy door behind her, and immediately the howling wind and biting air were replaced by the comfort and warmth in the Wilsons' foyer.

"Broderick—or Brody, as we call him—is already down for the night," Mrs. Wilson said. "He sleeps very well. I would be surprised if he woke once while we're gone."

"If you'd like to show me where your cleaning supplies are, Mrs. Wilson, I'd be happy to do some light housework while he sleeps."

"That won't be necessary. We have domestic help twice weekly. Besides, I would much prefer..."

A deep voice interrupted her. "Domestic help is just a fancy word for a maid."

I turned to the man descending the polished wooden staircase. "Mr. Wilson, I presume? I'm Emma."

"Chuck." He met me with a wink and a smile. "My father was Mr. Wilson." Placing an arm across Mrs. Wilson's shoulders, he said, "And now I do believe this hottie and I have a date."

Blushing, Mrs. Wilson pushed his arm away. "Goodness, Charles, it's an awards dinner for your law firm, not a date."

Mr. Wilson winked conspiratorially at me again. "Trinny's forgotten how to have fun, but I'll fix." Taking a more serious tone, he turned to Mrs. Wilson. "Just try to relax, sweetheart, and let's have a good evening.

Before leaving, Mrs. Wilson took me aside—out of Mr. Wilson's earshot—and laid out some very clear ground rules.

"Keep any noise to a minimum, Emma."

"I understand, Mrs. Wilson," I replied, but I was confused. She had, after all, told me that the baby slept well. Besides, the house was large, and his bedroom was upstairs. Any noise I made downstairs would be unlikely to reach him.

Her eyes searched mine intently. *I don't know if I can trust you*, they screamed. "Please, no noise," she almost pleaded.

I was beginning to feel uneasy, and I was about to ask her if there was something she needed to tell me when Mr. Wilson found us. "For Pete's sake, Trinity," he said, shaking his head, "it's going to be fine."

"First time with a babysitter?" I asked, trying to ease the discomfort.

Mr. and Mrs. Wilson both turned to me with unreadable expressions. "Something like that," Mrs. Wilson murmured.

An hour after they left, I was bored out of my mind. The silence in the home was overwhelming. I was tempted to turn on some quiet music, but the urgency in Mrs. Wilson's voice had shaken me.

Why is she so nervous? I wondered. I had been babysitting for a few years, but this was the first time I had encountered someone like Mrs. Wilson.

Standing and stretching, I decided to check on the baby. I climbed the stairs slowly, examining the family photos that were hung along the staircase. The portraits showed Mr. and Mrs. Wilson as a young couple holding hands in college, beaming at their graduation, wearing swimsuits on a beach somewhere tropical. Later pictures showed the couple at their wedding, then pregnant. After that, all the pictures included three family members: Mr. and Mrs. Wilson and a cute, chubby-faced baby boy.

I wondered at how motherhood affects people differently. It seems that most women take a shine to it, or maybe motherhood takes a shine to them, because they seem to smile a lot more and look a lot happier, even when they're getting much less sleep. Mrs. Wilson appeared to be the opposite. In her younger pictures, she appeared carefree, lighter somehow. Although she smiled in the photos with baby Brody, the expression wasn't quite genuine. There was a pall, a shroud of worry, of sadness that marred her expression.

Reaching the top of the stairs, I crossed the landing to the long hallway. It was apparent that the landing had at one time been open to the great room below, but it was now walled up. It seemed a shame to alter the originality of this beautiful old home by adding drywall to what must have been a wonderful open area to sit and read, but people do strange things.

Mrs. Wilson had told me that the baby's bedroom was the second door on the right down the hallway. "Please consider the other rooms off limits," she had instructed.

As I walked past the first door, a stark and sudden chill swept through me, ruffling my hair. *Yikes*, I thought, pulling my sweater snugly around myself. The window must have been left open, and wanting to save the Wilsons from an outrageous heating bill, I debated checking the inside of the room. Would Mrs. Wilson consider it a breach of trust? Then again, the hallway was so cold that the chill could seep down into the baby's room. Tentatively, I reached out and turned the knob, but my indecision quickly came to an end when I found that it was locked.

I shrugged and continued to the next door, surprised to feel that the chill did not continue past the first doorway. The door to the baby's nursery was open.

Baby Broderick was even cuter in the flesh than in his photographs. He was sleeping soundly, a thumb in his mouth, a dark lock of hair sweeping over impossibly long lashes. I reached out and swept the backs of my fingers against his smooth cheeks, wishing for a beauty product that could turn pimples and pores back into sweet infant smoothness.

After glancing around to make sure that everything was as it should be, I left the nursery. As I walked back down the long hallway, I noticed that the air outside the first doorway was no longer frigid.

Mr. and Mrs. Wilson had been gone less than two hours, and I was seriously considering abandoning my own set of rules when it came to babysitting. Never, and I do mean *never*, had I disobeyed parents' rules when watching their children, but Mrs. Wilson's frantic instructions bordered—no, crossed the line—on paranoia.

The shroud of absolute silence that had enveloped me for far too long was suddenly shattered by a voice behind me.

"Hi."

Never had such an innocuous statement startled me to the very core. I literally leaped off the couch and yelped out loud, spun around, and braced my arms defensively in front of me. My eyes landed on a young girl whose striking resemblance to Mrs. Wilson was the first thing I noticed. Speechless, I panted, my hand over my heart.

"Sorry." She giggled. "I didn't mean to scare you. Are you Emma?"

Still dumbstruck, I could only nod. Internally, my mind was trying to make sense of the person before me.

The girl plopped down on the couch next to me. "I'm Lona," she stated matter-of-factly, as though that should explain everything. She must have noticed my confused expression, and she added, "Lona Wilson. You're babysitting my brother."

Lona had long, dark hair like her mother, and the personality of her father. She explained that she had been at a neighbor's house earlier in the evening and had let herself in through her bedroom window. That explained why the hallway outside the first door had been so cold.

"I guess my parents didn't realize I was coming home," she said.

"Why didn't you just ring the doorbell?" I asked.

She shrugged, her shiny onyx hair falling over her shoulders. "My mother doesn't like noise," she said quietly, and for a moment, I saw her mother's sadness reflected in her own eyes.

"Lona," I said, wanting her to understand my sincerity, "it's not safe to be climbing the outside of your house to your window, okay? Your mom doesn't want you to get hurt, no matter what. Just ring the bell, okay?"

Lona smiled at me, the sadness not entirely gone. "Okay," she said.

* * *

My babysitting assignment for the Wilsons was much more enjoyable after Lona came home. I was surprised by how mature she was for ten years old. She had a wisdom about her that added years to her actual age.

Up in her room, now unlocked, she showed me her book collection.

"A lot of these are titles even I haven't read," I told her. "You must read a lot."

"I have a lot of time to read. That's what I do most of the time."

I pulled one of the books, *Little Women*, from its place on the shelf.

"That's one of my favorites," she said.

"I've never read it—"

"Brody needs me," Lona said, getting up from the carpet where she had been sitting cross-legged.

"I didn't hear him," I replied. I set down the book and followed after her.

Lona hurried into the room next to hers. Rounding the corner into the nursery, I saw her gently lift the baby from his crib. Sure enough, he was just beginning to rouse. Lona murmured quietly to her little brother, rocking him with an experienced hand.

"I'll go make him a bottle," I whispered.

Lona shook her head. "He won't need one. He just needs a little love from his sister, don't you, baby?" Rocking him a moment longer, she gave him a light kiss on his forehead and then returned him to his crib. The baby was again sound asleep.

"You really have a good instinct with him," I told Lona after we tiptoed back to her bedroom. "From what your mom told me about him being a deep sleeper, I wasn't expecting him to wake up at all. Good thing you were here to get him back to sleep."

Lona beamed at the compliment. "He actually wakes up all the time. I just soothe him before he disturbs my mother or father."

"That must be hard for you," I said, more and more impressed by this girl. "How do you get enough sleep?"

Lona shrugged. "I guess I just don't need as much sleep as my parents. Besides, it's my special time with my brother."

"I'm sure that you and Brody will have a special bond when he's older," I said.

Lona just stared at me in a way that unnerved me. "We'll see," she said. "I hope he'll know me."

I was about to ask her what she meant when I heard the door opening downstairs.

"I think your parents are home, Lona."

The sadness I had seen before swept back into her eyes like a tidal wave. She rushed forward and gave me a tight hug. Only then did I notice how cold she was.

"Where were you?"

Mrs. Wilson's expression bordered on frantic as I walked downstairs to greet them.

"For heaven's sakes, Trinny," Mr. Wilson said, "she was upstairs, doing what we're paying her to do, and doing a good job of it, I'm sure."

"That's right, Mrs. Wilson. Everything went just fine."

I could see the relief wipe the tension out of her, like a heavy wind finally releasing a clothesline from its torment.

"Oh, that's wonderful," she sighed. "And the baby, he's—?"

"He's sound asleep," I said. "He woke up once, but Lona knew exactly what to do to get him back to sleep."

"I... I... I'm sorry... What did you say?" the two of them looked at me in shock.

"Oh, I'm sorry," I said, "I forgot to mention that Lona came home while you were away."

"*Get. Out.*"

The words came out with such venom, such vitriol, it took a moment to register that they had been issued by the soft-spoken, timid Mrs. Wilson.

"I... uh... I..." I stammered, utterly confused.

"I said *get out*!" she wailed, this time in a pitch so loud it reverberated off the walls. "Get the hell out of my house!" She sobbed, collapsing against her husband.

Helplessly, I looked to Mr. Wilson. Surely Mrs. Wilson was having some kind of breakdown. Mr. Wilson's normally congenial face was now a mixed conflict of anger, hurt, and confusion. "Why, Emma?" he asked. "Why?" He pressed a handful of bills into my hand and said, "Please, just go."

Perplexed, enraged, and on the verge of tears, I walked out the door and let it slam shut behind me. It wasn't until I was at home and in bed that I realized I had left my phone at the Wilsons' house.

⁂

I woke up after a fitful night's sleep with the realization that something was seriously wrong in the Wilson home, and that whatever it was, Lona and her baby brother were smack in the middle of it. I remembered the sadness in Lona's eyes and the burden that she carried in caring for her brother. Then I thought about the family photos hanging in the stairwell. Something about the portraits had been bothering me, but I couldn't pinpoint what it was. Suddenly, it hit me: Lona wasn't in any of the photographs!

I jumped out of bed and hurried to dress, brush my teeth, and braid my hair. I was determined to confront Mr. and Mrs. Wilson, and getting my phone back was the least of my concerns at the moment.

The cold chill of the wind slapped my face as I ran the several blocks to their beautiful home. I arrived at their front doorstep, gasping for breath, but ready to demand answers.

Plik-a-plunk. That flat, nasally doorbell.

No answer.

Plik-a-plunk.

Still no answer.

I raised my fist and was about to begin banging on the door when it opened a crack. Mr. Wilson, looking much more subdued than the night before, peered out. "Emma, we thought we could expect you this morning." He opened the door wider. "Please, come in."

Hesitantly, I stepped inside and followed Mr. Wilson through the foyer into the living room. Mrs. Wilson, wrapped in a pink robe, sat with a cup of coffee on the couch, where Lona had scared me half to death the night before. "Good morning, Emma," she whispered.

"Good morning," I said.

"I suppose you came for this," Mr. Wilson said, holding out my phone, "but we have questions we'd like answered."

I regained some of my resolve, straightened my spine, and responded in what I hoped was a confident voice. "Yes, well, I also have some questions for you."

Regarding me as though I was a viper who might strike, Mr. Wilson asked in a low voice, "Emma, how did you know about Lona?"

This seemed like a strange question. "She came home from the neighbors' last night."

Mrs. Wilson responded to my reply with what sounded like a strangled whimper. Mr. Wilson scowled. "Emma," he said again, this time more firmly, "how did you know about Lona, and why did you say the things you said?"

"Why are you asking me this?" I shouted. "What is wrong with you?" Raising my voice, I asked again, "What is *wrong* with you? What kinds of parents make a ten-year-old responsible for a baby? What kinds of parents don't have pictures of their daughter in their house? What kinds of parents—" I stopped when I saw the stricken expressions on their faces.

"Oh, Lona. *Lona*!" Mrs. Wilson began to wail again.

Wrapping his arm around his fragile, shaking wife, Mr. Wilson looked at me. "Emma…" He paused to swallow a sob. "Lona's been dead for five years."

⁕

The Wilsons led me to the top of the stairwell, to the landing that I had noticed the night before.

"It used to be open to the lower level," Mr. Wilson explained. "Lona… she loved to read. She would sit on the railing to read. It was her favorite reading spot."

"I told her it was dangerous…" Mrs. Wilson said.

"She had a strong will," Mr. Wilson said, smiling. "It was one of the most wonderful things about her. And one of the most frustrating."

"The railing had just been waxed," Mrs. Wilson said. She stared off into the distance. "It was slippery."

"Trinity was downstairs in the kitchen," Mr. Wilson said.

"I was listening to music…" It was as though they were reliving the story in parallel universes, yet in sync.

"Lona slipped off the railing," he said. "She managed to catch herself and hang on. She was calling for help, but Trinity couldn't hear her."

"I couldn't hear her over the music." Mrs. Wilson wrapped her arms around herself and rocked back and forth. "Oh God, I couldn't hear her!"

"There was a break in the music, and Trinity heard her shouting for help," Mr. Wilson said. "She ran to her, but it was too late. She couldn't hold on any longer." Tears were running down Mr. Wilson's face. "Trinny tried to catch her, but she couldn't."

"I was too late. Oh God, I was too late," Mrs. Wilson moaned.

"I... I don't understand," I said. "She was here! She looks like you!" I pointed to Mrs. Wilson. "I sat with her in her room!"

Mr. and Mrs. Wilson looked at each other. "Emma, we keep her door locked," Mr. Wilson said.

I described Lona's room and its contents, down to the last detail of the books that were stacked neatly in her bookcase. Exchanging glances with his wife, Mr. Wilson withdrew a key from his pocket. The door creaked on its hinges as he pushed it open. The frigid air from inside hit me as soon as I stepped across the threshold, but the window was securely closed. Everything inside was coated with a thick layer of dust.

"Our housekeeper doesn't come in here," Mr. Wilson explained.

As I expected, the room was exactly as it had been last night, except for the coat of dust.

Stepping inside, Mrs. Wilson noticed the book that was lying open on the floor. "What's this?" she asked as she picked up the one item in the bedroom that was not covered in dust.

The title was *Little Women*.

This is my last time babysitting for the Wilsons. Brody is three years old now, and I leave for college next week. Even though we got off to a strange start, Chuck and Trinity—I mean Mr. and Mrs. Wilson—and Brody have become like a second family to me, and I'm going to miss them.

I turn off the kiddie movie we were watching, and I gather up Brody and his favorite stuffed animals for bed.

"I'm not sleepy," he says with a great big yawn.

I carry him up the stairs, feeling kind of sad that this will be my last time doing so. I walk slowly, gazing at the portraits that adorn the wall along the stairwell. Photos of Chuck, Trinity, Brody—and Lona.

"Lolo!" Brody says, pointing at the last photo taken of his sister.

"That's right, buddy," I say. "That's your sissy, and she loves you."

Lona hasn't made her presence known since that night three years ago, but I have no doubt that she's still here. Brody talks in his sleep a lot, and I've heard him say "Hi, Lolo!" more than once. His parents and I are sure that she is still rocking him back to sleep, and we think she'll continue to do so no matter how big he gets.

I tuck Brody in and read him his favorite bedtime story, then give him a kiss on his forehead just as his sister did the night I met her. I go downstairs, open a Coke, and get comfortable on the couch with a blanket and a good book. I'm deep in the storyline and oblivious to my surroundings when a familiar voice shatters the silence around me like it did one time three years ago.

"Hi!"

Meridian Man
by
David J. Lovato

Most people consider 12:00 AM to mark a new day. They're wrong. It's actually 6:42 PM, and I learned this the hard way.

People have been tracking time for as long as they've been aware of it. For as long as we've been able to think critically, we've been aware of its passage. We figured out how to observe it, measure it, try to contain it. But time can't be contained.

Regardless, our instruments have power. Sundials, shadows, watches, clocks, the gears that make them up, the metal and the glass; they're all attempts to harness something that can't be harnessed, only observed.

It takes a ritual. Don't ask me how I learned it. I went to unspeakable lengths. There were a hundred times along the way that I could've given up. I wish I had.

You find the spot where two walls meet and hang a clock on either wall, equidistant from the corner. Both must be precise; a nanosecond off and the whole thing doesn't work. And the corner has to be a perfect angle. Other than that, the details don't matter.

You stand twelve feet from the corner, facing it, staring into that spot where two walls meet, where two times meet, and at exactly 6:42 PM (Central Standard Time, by our constructs—not that those matter) the walls open up, and you go to that place between days.

It was like a drug trip, like the walls were being pulled apart before my eyes, the way walls slide away between scenes during a play. Then you're in the same space you were in before, but everything is off about it. Colors don't work properly, textures are all wrong. The air smells like sulfur, like something is constantly burning away. Maybe it is.

Time is frozen there. Or it doesn't exist. I can't explain it, and if I think about it too hard, my head hurts. My ears ring. Sometimes my nose bleeds. I have to get off that now.

At first I wandered for what felt like hours, in retrospect. It doesn't feel like anything there. Like I said, time either doesn't move or doesn't exist, so that ever-present awareness of its passage is gone. You just exist.

I was taking it in: the sights, the way light just doesn't seem to reflect off of anything properly, the way trees felt under my hand, smooth and almost giving to the touch, or how stones were prickly, how walking along the street felt like walking on a mattress. You could get lost there. I'm sure some have. But that didn't occur to me at the time, I was too proud of myself, too busy reaping the rewards of my research and labor. It never, ever occurred to me that I wasn't alone there.

I had noticed the lack of sound immediately—the air doesn't move, so how could anything make sound? Maybe that's why I heard it so easily, it was the only sound in existence: *Snip*.

I stopped moving, and almost lost my footing on that warped, malleable ground. I heard it again, a gentle, clean *snip*.

Curiosity got the best of me, and I made my way toward it. I could've walked for years for all I know. I crossed a lake, or maybe it was an ocean. You don't fall in; with time standing still, so does water. I walked and walked, like walking into the horizon, a horizontal line where two planes meet, much like the walls I'd taken to get here.

Finally, I saw the divider, the line that separates one day from the next.

It was glorious. How to describe it? Those walls that met were just walls, but next to this, an endless sky meeting an endless earth was just as plain. This was visible time, transparent blocks of passing seconds frozen still, one epoch pressed against another.

And, standing at the line where the two met stood a man. He was holding a pair of scissors, which he held to that line, carefully incising it: *Snip*. Hours or years or ages passed as he measured, aligned, inspected, then cut again: *Snip*.

I marveled at it for a while, just watching him work. Part of it was awe that there was someone else here, part of it was what he was doing. Where he cut the two days apart, they folded away, like the world, even with its depth, was cloth, fluttering in the wind, over a backdrop of starry night sky.

He was nearly finished cutting the days apart when I called out to him: "Beautiful!"

I could tell something was wrong by the way he suddenly froze. Slowly he turned to me, revealing himself. I had thought he was bald, but that's not quite right. It was almost like his skin didn't quite fit, like the whole thing was a loose-fitting blanket of flesh with holes cut in it long ago for arms and legs and eyes to get through. His face was less a face than a mask, and his eyes were yellow orbs, his mouth a fleshy snout, and no nose at all.

The look he gave me said *You're not supposed to be here*, and the feeling that followed it... "Dread" doesn't come close enough.

The pair of scissors in his hand clacked together, squeaking on their little metal hinge. Then he turned to me and lunged with them.

I more fell back than dodged, and those blades went past my shoulder. The scissorman let out a cry that was pain, anger, shock all at once as a new hole tore in the day. The backdrop behind this one wasn't night sky, it was a void blacker than black, it was the absence of existence, it was hell. From a few feet away I could feel it almost pulling at me, sort of like a gentle wind, or more like a powerful suggestion.

The anger in the scissorman's voice took over the other emotions, and he turned his burning gaze toward me again. I scrambled and ran.

You don't get physically tired there, but an emotional toll still comes from running for days, weeks, however long it was. I crossed mountains, I fled through empty cities, across frozen time with the scissorman at my heels. Those scissors cut through time itself, I couldn't bear to think of what they'd do to something so simple as me.

I had spent so long learning how to get there, I never bothered to wonder how I'd get back. I had plenty of non-time to think it over, and somewhere along the way, I had an idea.

Miles went by even if time didn't, at least not for anyone but me. Eventually I found my way back to where the scissorman had done his work, separating one day from the next. He had been so close to finishing, and I wasn't sure my plan would work, but I had to try. I just couldn't run anymore. Death would be a gift compared to

Scissor Man cuts, and
Scissor Man slices
Tendons and flesh, the
Scissor Man splices

He crafts a new hat,
nothing fancy about that
Aside from his
abhorrent vices

whatever those scissors would do to me, I knew that without a doubt. So I did the next best thing.

I reached that seam between days, two times floating in the wind, and I took one of them in each hand. If I could describe what it felt like to hold a day... Men would kill for that. Men would try to kill God for that. Even the scissorman didn't touch days with his bare hands; he used only his tool.

With time in my hands, I pulled them apart. The fabric tore, the days shredded with a shriek of pain and guilt and everything going wrong, or maybe it was the scissorman who made that sound. Maybe it was me. The two days came apart, free of each other with an explosion in my palms, a release of pressure and fear, and even then I saw my tear was jagged and frayed, not clean like the scissorman's cuts.

It was all over then. I stood facing that corner with those clocks, and saw the time was 6:42 and one second. I was back, I was safe.

I wish I could tell you the cost. Maybe you've noticed it, how time is a little off now. That tear, those frays, they aren't meant to exist. I've damaged time. I should've let the creature get me, should've accepted whatever punishment followed a swift click of those blades, but as always, I chose myself. What happens now? Maybe time and the universe and all existence slowly spin out of control, like a tear gradually growing larger, more unruly. All because I couldn't keep my hand out of the jar, because I tried to know the unknowable.

If the world doesn't break, I know my mind will. You don't really come back from a place like that. Not intact. I've begun to split in two, and now I'm only waiting for someone or something to come along and finish the job.

Out in the Woods
(Continued from page 92 X1-5)

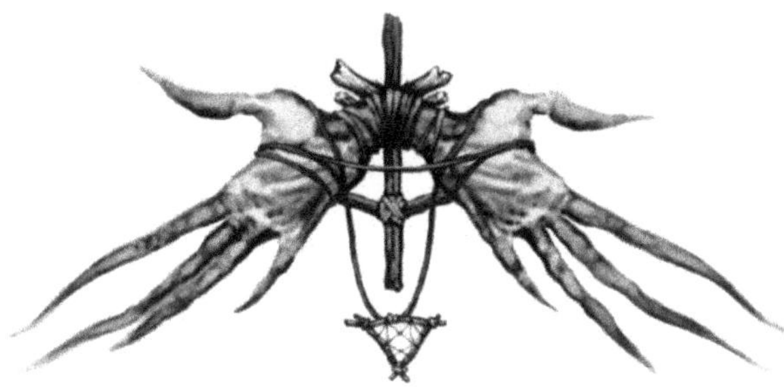

"Maybe we can get help and come back," Jessie said. The trio pressed onward. After a few minutes, they found the road.

"Which way are the cars?" Andy asked. They studied the scenery.

"This doesn't look familiar," Mark said. "They must be down that way."

It didn't take long to reach their cars. Mark's was closest, and all three got inside. Mark turned the key, and the engine roared to life, much to everyone's surprise. He turned around and headed toward town. Soon the forest road opened up into one of the main streets of the town, dotted by small business and offices, all dark and lifeless. They came to a red light and waited.

"The police station is up this way," Mark said.

"Good idea," Andy replied. They waited a little longer.

"...It's not going to change," Jessie said.

Mark lifted his head a little. "The phones. It's like... like time is frozen." He stepped on the gas and turned left, then slammed on the brake. Up ahead, fully illuminated by the streetlights and headlights, the bony woman stood in the road.

A calm but loud voice echoed in Jessie's head: *Get out of the car.*

Mark and Andy opened their doors and exited the car, which started rolling very slowly backward.

"What are you guys doing?" Jessie asked, but she realized she, too, had left the car.

Come to me, children.

Jessie wanted to scream at her friends to not listen to it, but instead she felt herself say, "She's calling."

Her legs moved on their own. She tried to still herself, back away, but instead she moved toward the creature. Her vision was full of fog, her ears were filling with white noise. To either side, the businesses lined the street, a taste of home so close, yet so utterly unhelpful.

Andy reached the gaunt woman first. Tentacles wiggled free from her back, white as her bones, and then shot forward, all but disintegrating Andy in an instant. Jessie wanted to scream, but couldn't even do that. Tears formed in her eyes.

The creature had barely finished with Andy when Mark stopped in front of her, and the tentacles wasted no time turning on him. Mark was gone in a cloud of red and white matter that made a tinkling sound as it splattered to the street.

Fuck you, Jessie thought.

It's okay, child, the creature replied. *I will bring you home.*

The white noise was deafening, the fog blocked most of her vision, but Jessie still saw the tentacles whip out toward her, felt them for only a split second, and then it was all over.

Crypto Bizarro

The Cost of a Haunted Doll
by
David J. Lovato

I'll admit I'm reluctant to sell this item on a website like this, but I can't get rid of it any other way. Nobody I know wants it, and I can't just throw it out. I apologize for the long item description, but telling the truth is the only way I can go through with it.

This item was given to me by a close friend a few months ago. She got it at a garage sale. She told me, as I suspect the previous owner told her, that the doll is haunted. My friend doesn't believe in ghosts but thought the doll was lovely, and it was only 25 cents (though you can see from the picture the doll is beautiful and looks like it's worth a lot more than that), so she bought it for me on the spot. I wasn't sure what to think at first. The eyes are the milkiest shade of blue I've ever seen, and the face is a creamy porcelain with rose red cheeks. Her hair is long and sandy blonde, and it doesn't feel artificial at all. They definitely don't make dolls like this anymore; I can only guess how old she is.

Still, there was something awfully creepy about the story behind it. But I was never too into ghost stories either, and thought it would make a great gift for my daughter.

She immediately didn't like it. She said it was creepy, that it looked like it was watching her. I told her there was nothing wrong with the doll, so she should just relax and in time she'd come to like it. I set it on the shelf facing her bed.

My daughter didn't get any rest the first night. She had night terrors, something that has never happened before. At one point she started screaming and wouldn't stop. My husband and I tried everything to get her to calm down, but she wasn't even coherent. Then, out of nowhere, she quit screaming. We were worried, and she still wouldn't talk, she just stared off into space. Finally she just said, "The lady is gone, I can go back to sleep now."

We wanted to ask her what she meant, but she hit the bed like a rock after that, and we didn't want to risk waking her again, so we just went back to sleep.

The next day she said she felt sick. I told her she could stay home from school, and her eyes widened and she said she felt fine after all and wanted to go. After some arguing I finally relented and let her go, thinking it a bit weird.

My husband works and I'm retired, so I spend a lot of time buying junk, fixing it, and selling it here on this site. It's a nice hobby and it keeps me from going insane with boredom. I get started on this just about every day after my daughter goes to school.

On that day I nearly had a heart attack while, when digging through a box of stuff I had collected, I found the doll. At first I thought I must've already bought the same model, but I know I would've remembered a doll as beautiful as this. So I took the doll and rushed upstairs to my daughter's bedroom, and sure enough the doll was not on her shelf.

I put it back and went downstairs to continue working. I figured she must've moved it sometime during the night. At dinner I asked her about it, but she swore she didn't touch it, and in fact *wouldn't* touch it. We argued again, after which she went to bed crying, and I felt terrible.

The next morning, after she went to school, I got started with my work. I again found the doll in a box. Furious, I put it on her shelf and went back downstairs. An hour or so later I sat down at my computer to type up an item description; I all but screamed when I saw the doll sitting on the couch across the room, staring right at me. I knew I put it back upstairs and no one else was home, so how it got there was beyond me.

I'm a reasonable person, but after two more days of my daughter having night terrors and me finding the doll in strange places, I thought about how the doll was supposedly haunted. I just couldn't rule that out anymore.

I decided to get rid of the doll. I wouldn't force my daughter to keep it in her room, instead I tossed it into the basement, in a box under the stairs, until I could sell it.

The next morning, my daughter woke up screaming. The doll was in its first spot, on her shelf, smiling giddily at her.

I threw the doll away. I put it in a trash bag, tied it up, and took it out to the curb. I kept my eyes glued to the bag from the window until the garbage truck came.

It was sitting at the foot of my bed when I woke up the next morning.

That afternoon I was washing the dishes. I was doing a sinkful of bowls and plates, which always followed the silverware. I felt a sharp pain and when I pulled my hand from the soapy water, it was bleeding. For some reason, there was a serrated knife in the sink. I figured I must've missed one, until I turned around to get a bandage and saw the doll sitting on the floor in the kitchen entryway.

After I finished the dishes, I drained the sink, put the doll in it, poured lighter fluid all over it and set it on fire. I watched the doll burn, and I smashed it with a hammer to get rid of the porcelain that didn't. The whole time it watched me with its milky blue eyes.

When it was reduced to little more than ashes, I washed them down the drain. I didn't tell my husband or daughter anything except that we wouldn't have to worry about the doll anymore.

The next morning, my little girl said she said she saw the lady again. She said this lady was very small, very old, and had only one eye in the center of her face. The lady spoke to her and told her that Mommy had done something very bad. Then she went away. I told my daughter not to worry about it, and I sent her to school anyway. I'll admit that it bothered me.

Later that day I received the phone call. My husband was in a car wreck on his way home from picking up our daughter. The police said it was the worst wreck they had ever seen. The only thing they were able to pull from the car was a doll that didn't have a scratch on it. I took it when they offered it back to me. I knew it would end up here anyway.

Now I'm getting rid of this item the only way I know for sure works. I'm selling it. I really just couldn't bring myself to do it without telling the truth. I'm hoping someone out there on the internet knows something, some way to get rid of this doll, some way to destroy it. Or maybe someone won't believe my story, and will buy it anyway.

In any case, I wish the best of luck to all bidders.

Of Mice and Monsters
by
Josh Leichliter

Megan loved her new house. It was a modest but recently remodeled Victorian that she adored. Her new neighborhood was too good to be true: Her property faced a large, lush park with ponds and streams, trees, and playgrounds. Children played while their parents gossiped away the warm summer evenings.

After an exhausting day of unpacking, Megan went to her porch and plunked down into a cozy wicker chair, rewarding herself with a frosty glass of Chardonnay. She had squirreled away cash for ten long years for this house. The scenery was breathtaking, especially compared to the ghetto she had just moved from. "Too good to be true," she confirmed aloud. Megan closed her eyes, settled in with a smile, and quickly drifted off to sleep.

"Hey!"

Megan awoke sluggishly to the sound of a man hollering. "Hey," he snapped again. His weirdly high-pitched voice jolted her awake. She sat up in her chair and blinked, her eyesight slowly coming to focus. It was dark now, but she could just make out the figure of a man standing in the shadows, near the sidewalk.

"Uh, hi?" Megan answered, perplexed.

"You're new."

"Yeah, hi," Megan said, carefully masking her uneasiness. "I'm Megan. I just moved in."

The man waited a few moments, then responded, sourly, "I know. I'm Walt. I live down the street. I'm watching you." His darkened face split into a spidery grin, followed by a snorting sort of laughter. "I'm the neighborhood watch, y'see. Bad things happen at night, ya know. Be safe. Bye-bye!" The last part he sang with tangible sarcasm, sending shivers up Megan's spine. With that, he turned and slowly wandered off, remaining among the shadows of the towering spruces.

Megan watched him go, startled by the whole encounter. After a dozen steps or so, he reached a pool of streetlight, stopped, and turned around. He stared back at her with that same spidery grin. She covered her mouth to suppress her gasp when his grotesque, leathery face came into focus. His skin was pale and

Zbryfzx ybwhd td ctzk doejord td ryo vbrrbc bg ryo dot.

blotchy, and his proportions were all wrong. He lazily lifted a bulbous, deformed arm and waved at her. With that, Megan rose quickly and stepped inside, locking the door behind her.

The next evening, Megan was shopping at the local supermarket when she received a phone call.

"Hello?"

"Yer curtains are lovely, Megan. Look forward to seeing you!" Walt's overly cheerful, high pitched tone made her feel sick as she quickly hung up the phone. She hadn't given him her number, and she certainly didn't want to see him again. His interest in her curtains was especially disturbing. She hurried home and unloaded the groceries as fast as she could. She didn't see him, but she felt like he was there, watching her from the shadows.

Megan awoke on Tuesday to a loud banging sound outside. It was 6:33 in the morning. She drew back the curtains to see Walt going through her trash cans. He had knocked one over, and was digging through another. Enraged, Megan called the police. Walt was three houses down when they caught up with him, going through a neighbors' trash. He claimed he was looking for cans to recycle. The police found no cans, nor anything else suspicious on him, so they released him with a warning.

Megan glared at him as he walked past her, presumably on his way home. He simply cracked his familiar arachnid smile, waved his flabby arm lazily, and said "Sorry 'bout that, Miss Megan. Won't happen again."

For the rest of the day, every little sound had Megan on edge. She half expected Walt to be lurking around every corner.

Wednesday was a good day. Megan was settling into her new house, and she hadn't heard a thing from Walt all day. It seemed his run-in with the police had scared him off, for now at least. His erratic, escalating behavior was beginning to scare her, and she was considering filing a restraining order against him. He had done nothing overtly wrong, though she was certain he was stalking her. He probably wanted to murder her, or God knows what else! She shuddered, and forced the morbid thoughts from her mind.

Megan decided to focus on the positive. She loved her new house, and couldn't wait to show it off. She'd invited her best friend Rosalia over for girls' night, planning to indulge in liberal wine and some inebriated final-touch decorating. Megan hummed cheerfully as she tapped nails into the walls with her cute pink hammer. She hung pictures of her family and friends, and some of her favorite artwork.

The doorbell rang, Rosalia was here early! Megan skipped to the door and threw it open with a smile. "Rosie!"

Megan was shocked to discover Walt standing there instead. "Hi, Megan." He grinned menacingly.

"Walt, what the hell are you..." She hadn't even finished her sentence when Walt suddenly thrust his hand into his tattered jacket. Megan caught a glint of metal and screamed. Her vision blurred as she reacted on instinct, lashing out like a cornered animal. With a sickening thump, Walt's head snapped back, and he collapsed to the porch, a blackish pool of blood ebbing from his broken skull like some carnal halo.

Megan was completely confused as to what had just happened, when a sickly feeling began to swell in her stomach. She glanced at her hands and realized she was still holding her pink hammer, now red with gore.

Megan threw her hand over her mouth, gasped, and dropped the hammer. She stared in horror at the convulsions of the ugly old man. His hands and legs thrashed as his damaged brain attempted to reboot. Megan saw the familiar flash of metal as he convulsed. It wasn't a weapon, just a greeting card wrapped in garish silver foil, now creased and blotted with Walt's blood. Walt had welcomed her with a greeting card, and she had thanked him with a hammer to the head.

Seconds ticked like hours. Dumbfounded she stood, trying to fully comprehend her situation. Megan's world began to crash down around her. In a fit of impunity she had attacked the old man, and now he lay on her porch, dying. Everything she had worked so hard for would be gone. She would spend the rest of her life in prison. "No, no..."

Half-dazed, Megan sat down and calmly called Rosalia to cancel girls' night. Embarrassed, she apologized, rescheduled, and hung up. Then she went to the kitchen and put on a pair of rubber gloves.

Dragging Walt's still twitching body to the kitchen was a considerable effort, but she eventually managed. Megan quietly shut the front door, covered her mouth, and raised her cute pink hammer. She would get messy tonight.

Out in the Woods
(Continued from page 105 X2-2)

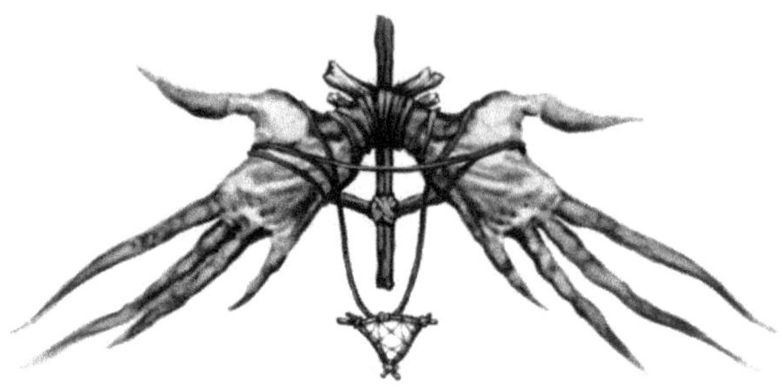

Melissa lay a few feet away. Jessie left the phony security of her sleeping bag and crawled over to her. "Hey," she said. Jessie nudged her friend. "Melissa, wake up."

"What?"

"My phone's not working. Look."

Melissa squinted, blinded by the light of the phone, then rolled away from Jessie. "Go to sleep, Jessie."

"Something's freaking me out. I think there's an animal or something nearby."

"Jessie, quit it. You're scaring me."

"Listen."

The girls stayed quiet, but the woods were silent, and nothing moved.

"Jessie, it's nothing. Go back to sleep."

Reluctantly, Jessie lay back down, but sleep wasn't going to happen. Her heart was pounding, and every second felt like hours, especially with no working clock. Now and then she checked to see if anyone else was awake, but found only the surrounding trees. She checked her phone: 1:44. Her stomach was a pit. She looked away from her phone, let her eyes adjust to the darkness, then noticed Mark standing up a few feet from his sleeping bag.

"Mark," Jessie whispered. "You okay?"

"She's calling," Mark said.

"What? Who? Is your phone working?"

Mark pointed into the trees. Jessie squinted, and then she saw it.

Between the trees, barely distinguishable from them, a figure stood. It was tall, with a round, bald head, and Jessie's heart entered free-fall as the rest of it came into focus. Whatever it was had no skin, and stood naked and bony, slender and feminine in the moonlight. Its bones were warped, with thick ridges running along them, like the trunks of trees.

The creature lifted her arms, as if to embrace someone. Mark started toward her.

"Mark!" Jessie whispered.

"She's calling," Mark said.

Jessie stood up and shouted. "Who are you? What do you want from us!"

Mark took another step toward the bony woman as the others around him started to stir.

"Stop!"

Jessie ran toward Mark, but he had already reached the edge of the clearing, and was only a few feet from the bony woman. Had she gotten closer?

The darkness at the edge of the clearing changed. Jessie stopped in her tracks as long, tentacle-like appendages grew out of the bony woman and the ground around her. They writhed silently, now and then showing white in the moonlight, the same bony texture as the rest of the woman. Then they lashed forward, grabbing Mark and pulling him closer, before ripping him apart like tissue paper. Blood splashed the surrounding grass and trees, Jessie covered her eyes as it flecked her face, heard the embers of the campfire sizzle quietly at a drop or two.

When Jessie let her arm down, the bony woman was gone. Steph was screaming, trying to run toward the mess of red and pinkish matter, but Andy held her back.

John took out his phone, Melissa started crying. Leaves rustled, and she jerked her head to look.

"I can't get into my phone," John said.

"I can't either," Jessie replied.

Everyone had the same problem Jessie did: the phones wouldn't unlock, and were all stuck at 1:44 AM. Only Melissa's was different, it was stuck at 1:45.

"So... what do we do?" Andy said.

"We have to get out of here," Steph said. She sniffed hard and wiped at her eyes. Jessie wrapped her arms around her, and Steph hugged her back.

John limped over to his bag and opened it. He dug around for a second, then got out his flashlight. He tossed it to Andy, who caught it out of the air, turned it on, and pointed it around.

"Which way did we come from?"

Jessie took the flashlight and pointed it. "That way."

"We don't have the GPS," Steph said.

"If we go in a straight enough line, we can still reach the road. We just might take a little longer to get there."

"You sure that's the way?" John asked.

Jessie looked around. Every tree jumped at her, the flashlight barely cut through the fog, and that rain or wind sound, like some kind of mind haze, was louder than before.

"Yeah, I came straight to this log," Melissa said. "From over there. And you went down to the creek right that way, remember?"

"Yeah."

Calm and booming, louder than her own thoughts, Jessie heard a voice.

Children. Come to me. Come to Mother.

The looks on her friends' faces told her they heard it, too. Melissa was the first to start running in the direction they'd settled on, and the rest soon followed.

Jessie had the flashlight, so she soon took the lead. Every tree that popped into the light made her heart skip a beat, every branch could be one of the creature's appendages. Jessie ran faster. When she looked back, she saw Andy and Steph, but no Melissa or John. She stopped.

"Where are the others?"

"Shit!" Andy said. "John's leg!"

"We have to go back," Steph said. Andy was leaning his hands on his legs, catching his breath. He looked up. "We'd be going toward that... thing."

"Jessie?" Steph said.

To keep going, turn to page X2-2-1 (154).
To go back for the others, turn to page X2-2-2 (55).

Crypto Bizarro

Axis
by
David J. Lovato

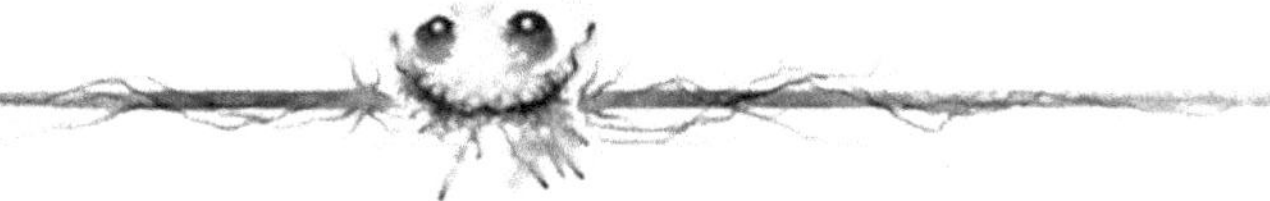

Everyone can be an angel .liveb a ʇo
We're all capable of doing amazing things, ,ꙅꙅoɹɹoɥ ǝldɒmoɥʇɒʇnu
ǫniɥꙅilqmoɔɔɒ
Improving the world, ,nwob ʇi ǫniuɹud
Having an impact on ǫnibnǝ someone else's life.
You hold the power in your hands ʇɒoɹɥʇ ɹǝbnǝʇ ɒ ǝʞil
To fly in that blue sky. .bǝɹ ni ꙅllɒw ǝɥʇ ʇniɒq oʇ
It all starts ꙅbnǝ with you.
Just look in the mirror.
.ɹoɹɹim ǝɥʇ ni ʞool ʇꙅuႱ

alert. Stay
Do not panic.

alert. Stay
Do not panic.

tay awake
o not panic

Stay
awake.
Stay

The Joker
by
Andrea Wright

"Call it!" snarled the big hairy man with death breath.

How did I get myself into this mess? And why is this guy being so mean?

Serpio watched the man's glinting eyes, then looked at the coin he was holding in his bulky, cracked hand. He could tell this man was serious. "I really don't care for this!" Serpio said.

"Call it!" the hairy man stomped and glowered, causing a sudden hush to fall over the other patrons. Metal cups hanging from the ceiling clinked and swayed.

"All right!" Serpio stepped back, sweating. "I call tails!"

The hairy man flipped the coin up in the air. It turned and spun, until the hairy man's hand whipped out and snatched it. He slapped it on the back of his other hand and slowly revealed the face of the coin. Serpio let out his breath as he realized it was tails. He'd won the call. He'd better think of a joke— fast! Looking around the room, he hoped for something to jog his brain. He saw a wooden floor, a rough cut bar, animal heads on the walls, a dozen faces staring at him. All he'd wanted was a quick lager, and this hole-in-the-wall place seemed as good as any. Sure, one beer had turned into five, but he felt he deserved it. It had been a hard day.

He wasn't a thief all the time, just when he really wanted something and decided that by all rights it should be his. And after all, that little girl had approached *him* first. She'd been so drawn to the beautiful scarf that he had acquired a while back and now hung off his belt. "Please, sir," she'd said, "Can I look at it?" Her eyes grew wide as the swirls and colors drew her in. She put her hand in her pocket and drew out a handsome coin. "Can I buy it? Daddy says I can buy something for me birthday."

Now where did she get a coin like that? Suddenly he had a mad desire to have it, and of course he wouldn't part with the scarf. Before he knew it, he had grabbed her hand. Her little fist clenched tight. "No!" she cried. Too bad. It didn't take much for him to pry open her hand and take it. Sorry about her poor little wretched fingers.

As she cried and ran away, he chuckled and called after her. "Hey, it was just a joke!"

Now all he wanted to do was pay his tab and go home. When he laid the coin on the bar, a huge, crazed-looking man promptly stomped over. His beard was long and scraggly, and he was covered from the waist down in dried mud. The hairy man snatched the coin and demanded a game of Heads or Tails. "Joke or Death!" he snarled angrily.

Serpio was not a funny man, and could not think of a joke just now. Mr. Hairy withdrew a large cleaver from his overcoat, and with a dull thud, buried it into the bar top. Serpio screamed when he realized his hands were on the other side of the blade.

"Oops, just kidding! Ha ha!" Bellowed the stranger, as he flipped the handsome coin into the air. His little girl caught it with a snap, and a smile on her face.

"Wanna hear a joke, Daddy?"

Shanghai
by
Nick Brown

San Francisco, 1921

Shanghai they taught me, and shanghai I must!
Under the bars I caught them, and out the docks I tossed.
I did so good I'm rotten! You can see it in their eyes, so lost.
Shanghai they taught me, and shanghai I must!

145

Alone
by
David J. Lovato

Dry, dead leaves crackled beneath my feet with every step. My Chucks mashed them into the ground, breaking them into tiny bits that might become part of the earth, fertilize other trees, keep these woods alive. But the satisfying crunch was the real reason I'd go out of my way to step on those big, orange leaves, sometimes taking two steps to get to the crunchiest-looking ones.

These hikes were what kept me alive. The woods entrance was down the street from my house, so I could come here any time, even in the middle of the night, like now. I preferred the nights; hardly anyone ever came up here, and if they did, we'd maybe wave or smile and then pass each other, and I'd be alone again. But sometimes even that's too much, and at night, the woods were always mine.

My headlamp beam started to flicker. *Crunch crunch crunch.* It went out entirely.

"Damn it."

I took it off and fumbled through the dark for some batteries in my bag. As my eyes adjusted, I realized I could still see. In the distance, what looked to be a few meters off of the trail, something was glowing.

I finished switching out my batteries, pulled my hair back, and slid the headlamp back on. I started toward the glow, turning the light off every few steps to make sure I was going the right way.

It wasn't too far ahead, a little off the trail, just up a small but steep hill. I started up, using the trunks of tiny trees for balance, angling my feet so I wouldn't slip. The hill evened out, and I turned off my lamp as I made my way between larger trees toward the glow. It was small and yellow, but the woods were so black, it could probably be seen for a mile. Finally I broke into a clearing, and sitting on the leaf of a small plant was a little yellow orb, glowing brightly, slowly pulsating.

What in the world? I thought. I'd seen all kinds of plants and wildlife out here, but never anything like this. I took my phone out, opened up the camera, and snapped a few pictures. A more popular girl would probably take them straight to social media. Hell, I knew I'd be posting it on Instagram later, but with few-to-no followers, I was in no hurry. It's not like anyone cared what I had to show or say anyway.

Part of me expected the orb to not show up on camera, but there it was. I decided to go in for a closer shot, and I moved the camera in close, a few millimeters away from the orb. That's when it jumped. The sphere elongated for a second, then it was on my fingers, just below my camera. Startled, I pulled back, dropped my phone. The thing slithered up my hand. I swiped at it, trying to pull it off, but my hand only glided over the thing. It felt like velvet, soft and almost furry, but it was like trying to wipe peanut butter away. The thing would only stretch very slightly in the direction I wiped, all the while making much more progress up my arm.

"No! Get off!" I wiped harder, smacked at it, shook my arm, and then it was on my shoulder, then my neck, then I felt it slither into my ear. Did I scream? I don't even know. My sight went golden, then everything was blurry, fading into pitch black, I landed on my knees, and then everything was gone.

I woke up in my bedroom. For a second I didn't remember anything, and then it occurred to me that I didn't remember coming home. That's when memories flooded in. I sat up quick, felt my ear, felt my face, but everything seemed fine. I looked at the clock; I needed to start getting ready for school.

I sat alone on the bus, and again at lunch. It's one of those things you tell yourself you don't mind doing, but really you do. I mean, everyone wants to be alone sometimes, but not many people want to always be alone. Anyway, it's not like I had a choice.

I saw Sarah coming up to me. She was an acquaintance; we talked a lot, but I couldn't really call her a friend. We never hung out outside of school, and she wouldn't sit with me at lunch or anything, but it was nice to see her.

"Hey," she said. She stopped beside me, holding her tray, scanning the cafeteria for her friends.

"Hey," I replied.

"What's with that picture you posted last night?"

"What?"

"On Instagram. The plant."

I put my fork down, took out my phone, opened the app. Sure enough, there was that photo I took: A little green plant, the glowing orb on its leaf. The post was adorned with hashtags: #love #unity #together #peace.

"I... don't remember posting this. But I took it last night, out in the woods."

"What is it?"

"I don't know." I wanted to tell her about how it attacked me, but that would be weird. "You'll find out soon enough." I slapped my hands to my mouth. What did that even mean? Why did I say it?"

"What?"

"Nothing. I don't know. Sorry."

"You okay, Amber?"

"I think so. Sorry. I didn't sleep enough."

"Well, let me know if you need anything."

"Thanks, Sarah." She headed off to eat with her friends. What was all of this about?

It's strange how things take precedence over others in your brain. Here I was worrying about glowing orbs, lacking memories, and saying things I had no intention of saying, and my whole world still came to a silent halt when Kyle Gibbons entered my line of sight. I watched him walk, one of his ear buds dangling out of his ear. I liked that about him; sometimes he disappeared into his music, but he often left one out, his ear exposed to the world, open, approachable. And almost entirely unaware that I existed. I mean, maybe we were as close as me and Sarah, but Kyle would never go out of his way to talk to me. I'm sure I meant nothing to him, just another face in the crowd.

He passed by, and everything started moving again: The world started spinning, I finished eating, and I wondered what the hell had happened to me last night.

I ate dinner with my mother that night. She asked me about my day, about my life, and I mostly nodded or shook my head. She tried, and I loved her more than anything, but sometimes you don't need to be reminded about how lonely you are, how every day is exactly the same.

"Anything exciting happen?"

"No. Not really."

"Well, what are your plans for this weekend?"

I shrugged. She started saying something about her day, but all I could focus on was my fork. A piece of chicken dangled from it, and I was hungry, suddenly more hungry than I'd ever been, or maybe just more focused on it, but I couldn't move. What was wrong with me? My hand was shaking a little.

I put down my fork. *Why?* I got up from the table. *What?* I walked through the opening into the living room, where the TV was on to some crafting channel, and I switched it over to the news.

"—strange fungus have appeared without explanation in several cities. The CDC has assured us there appears to be no danger from the bioluminescent plants."

There on the TV was the little yellow orb I'd seen, dozens of them on different plants and in different video quality. I wasn't the only one who had seen it. I watched myself take out my phone, scroll to another picture I'd gotten, a close-up (when had I even taken it?), and posted it with the hashtag *Soon*.

"Amber? Are you all right?"

"Yes, mother." What was *that*? That isn't how I talk. I walked slowly back to the dinner table and finished my food, but it was like I was dreaming, maybe sleepwalking, barely participating in my own life at all.

The next day at school, something exciting certainly happened. I was walking through the hall, hall pass in hand, on my way to the girls' bathroom. Ahead, Kyle Gibbons rounded the corner. I flinched, hoped he hadn't seen, gathered myself, and carried on. When we got close, I waved. "Hey, Kyle!"

"Hey, Amber. What's up?"

"Not a lot," I said. Then I stepped to the side, in front of him, blocking his path. What was I doing?

Kyle smiled a little. "Sorry," he said, and stepped aside, but I stepped along with him, preventing him from moving. "Shall we dance?" He laughed, and I laughed, then took a step toward him. My heart was racing, some of it excitement, some of it fear. "I should really get back to class, Amber."

"What's the rush?" I put my hands on his chest, looked around with exaggerated movement. "Nobody's out here but us."

"What are you doing?"

Words almost forced their way out of my mouth, but I pushed harder, concentrated, and said, "I don't know. I'm sorry." Then fear took over as something else did. I moved on my own, wrapping my fingers around his neck, pulled him down slightly, and kissed him. What was happening to me? I wanted to scream, even as his tongue grazed mine, as my fingers wove through his hair like I knew they never would have, never should have, if not for these sudden outbursts, like someone else was controlling me.

My heart was beating faster than I thought possible, until he put his hands on my sides, relaxed a little. In my mouth I felt something, but was it just his tongue? Maybe mine? No, it felt like something else, something starting at the back of my throat and moving forward, but then it was gone, and suddenly I let go, stepped back, away from him, away from what I always wanted—

But not like this.

Kyle coughed, cleared his throat, put his hand on the back of his neck, looked away. "Look, Amber... that was fun. I don't really know you that well though. It was kinda weird."

I don't know what came over me, I thought. But what I said was "You'll get used to it, in time."

"What?"

"Soon." Then I started walking away, and no matter how hard I tried, I couldn't stop moving, couldn't look back, couldn't do anything but scream in my head.

<hr>

The next day I was on full autopilot. There was no emotion to anything I did: Open my eyes. Stand up. Go to the bathroom. Brush my teeth. Brush my hair. Tie my shoes. Go to school. My eyes were dry, but my chest was heavy, my throat was twisting, I wanted to cry, wanted to scream, wanted to do anything at all.

I made out with three more boys and Sarah, that day. I don't know why. I think I stopped paying attention, for the most part. It was an hour after school, and I was making out with Bradley Jones in the boys' locker room when I sort of snapped out of it, or at least back into my own mind. Bradley, who had always had kind of a thing for me, looked concerned. He wiped a tear from my eye. "You okay?"

"Yeah. I think I should go home." Did I say that, or did *I* say that?

"Okay. Sorry."

"It's fine. See you tomorrow."

Leaves crunched beneath my feet as I walked. It was a half hour trip, a little shorter if I took the path by the railroad tracks, but for once I was in control, I was moving my feet, so I went the longer route. I even almost smiled as I went out of my way to step on a big, brown, dried leaf.

Is it really all that bad?

I stopped walking. That thought was in my voice, but I hadn't thought it.

What are you? What are you doing to me?

Making you whole. Come now, don't act like you don't enjoy it. Their tongues on yours, their hands on your breasts. You'd never have this if not for me.

"What are you talking about?" I said aloud. Then my mouth closed, and I grunted, tried to open it, put both hands to my lips and tried to pry my own mouth open.

Peace. Love. Unity. Finally. For all of you. A gift.

The tone was gentle, soothing. And I realized I was walking, I was almost home. I was crying.

Just leave me alone.

I could make you jump out in front of a bus. I could make you sit at the bottom of a lake. Yet all I want to do is make you feel love. And you ask me to stop?

This is me. My body, my mind.

I laughed out loud.

The next day, most of the school was making out, even teachers. A few people looked concerned, some asked questions. They always ended up surrounded, carried off to privacy. Some of them screaming.

Over the next few days, everyone started acting strange. Everyone woke up on time, traffic flowed perfectly. We went to school, took our seats, listened to our teachers, learned everything. The news was mostly weather, commercials disappeared *Hsj'l yoaju, cjh lipj cpsijh qosgob. ...nchv bsi ossu.* from TV and radio. No one paid for anything, everyone did their jobs. All of the wars ended.

I couldn't stop screaming inside. That's all I did. I couldn't form thoughts as words very often, and when I did, that other thing inside me pushed them away.

I was lying awake in the early hours of Saturday morning, a passenger in my own body, when I felt a tear roll down my cheek. I savored it; it was precious, the first thing in a long time that was actually mine.

Oh, come now. There is peace, there is love. You never have to be alone again. Do you want Kyle? He can be beside you in minutes.

I realized I could think. The thing was letting me reply.

Not like this.

There is no other way. You think he would ever love you? You think the world could ever be so complete on its own? That soldiers would set down their arms, that your kind would stop fighting over lines on maps? All on their own?

At least we could try.

The thing laughed. I cried. Soon Kyle entered my room, and together we moved perfectly, loved perfectly, and nothing ever hurt so much in my life. I could see it in his eyes, the same thing I felt: Trapped.

On Sunday, all of the churches filled up. We didn't read from any books, there was no pastor or sermon, just all of the people, gathered together in perfect harmony, a silent worship of this thing that had taken over all of mankind, this thing worshipping itself, keeping itself going, convinced it was doing it for our benefit.

The world spun on. We all walked along in our slavery, our forced utopia. I was walking home from school one day, who even knows what day, when a leaf crunched beneath my feet, and I stopped.

Maybe the thing was somehow asleep, or taking a break, or maybe it was just controlling so many people that it had a momentary lapse, but whatever the case, I was in control. Tears poured from my eyes and I sobbed heavily, but I covered my mouth. I was afraid it would hear. I looked around. What could I do? I was staring at the railroad tracks.

The thing sounded afraid when it came back, fear in my own voice.

Amber, what are you doing?

I smiled, lying there, staring up at the sky. I shivered hard; the thing wanted its control back. I would fight until I couldn't fight any more.

Amber, this solves nothing.

The tracks started to rumble beneath my back.

Amber, please. Get up. Don't do this.

"They need to know," I said. I could hear the train screeching to a halt. It wouldn't matter. It was too late.

Know what? Amber, just take my gift. You won't ever be alone.

"They need to know they can fight you. And you know what? They'll win."

For what? More wars? More famine, more people taking everything and leaving others with nothing? More boys ignoring you in the hall? A life of solitude, Amber?

"Yeah, I was alone," I said. "Even unhappy. But I was me. Not you. And I could've been anything, someday."

The screeching was deafening, the urge to get up and run astounding. I fought with every fiber of my being to lie there, to escape, to be free again.

Then I felt the release, I felt myself become whole again, wholly mine. I leapt to my feet, dove forward, and covered my head as the train blared on past me, no longer coming to a stop. I don't know how long I lay there after it passed, and the world grew silent except for the wind.

Go then, the thing said. *Be alone.*

And I would, but not for long. Those other people are still in there somewhere. And we can fight. We can free ourselves. That's what we do. We're never alone.

Out in the Woods
(Continued from page 138 X2-2-1)

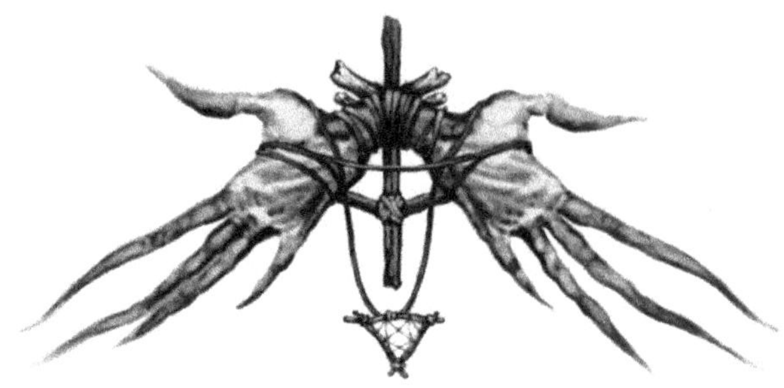

"We can come back with help," Jessie said. She, Andy, and Steph pressed on. A few minutes later, they reached the road.

"Where are the cars?" Andy asked. Jessie studied the scenery.

"I think we're up the road from where we parked," Steph said. "None of this looks familiar."

"I think you're right," Jessie said. The trio headed down the road, and soon Jessie's flashlight bounced off of a reflector. Their hearts raced, and Jessie almost even smiled as they reached Mark's car, with Melissa's a few yards behind, but their hope quickly died.

"Fuck," Jessie said. "Steph, please tell me you have a key to your brother's car."

"God damn it," Steph said.

"We should've gone back," Andy said. "I'm sorry."

Jessie shook her head. "It's not your fault. We have to go back now anyway." She turned around and froze.

In the middle of the road stood the bony woman. Her gaunt face displayed a smile in the glow of a nearby streetlight, she stared into Jessie's soul with pitch black eyes.

Children. I told you to come.

"She's calling," Andy said.

"Ignore her," Jessie said, but she couldn't take her eyes off of the bony woman. When did all that fog set in?

Children. Come to Mother.

Jessie's legs moved on their own. She tried to stop, tried to look away, and instead only dropped her flashlight. It shattered on the road.

The woman stood ten feet away. Some of her ridges writhed and came to life, tentacles protruded all around her and flailed in the air.

Steph reached her first. The vine-like bones lashed out and tore her apart, painting the asphalt red. She had barely finished with Steph when Andy stopped before her, and the tentacles wasted no time in reducing him to a cloud of blood and organ matter.

It's okay, child.

Jessie felt the blood squish beneath her shoe. Those black eyes called to her, the open arms seemed so welcoming. Then the tentacles whipped forward, and it was all over.

On a Rural Highway
by
Josh Leichliter

Jack slammed Bobby's face into the car hood, cracking his two front teeth. Bobby cried out at the impact, his mouth bleeding from the injury. "I swear Jack," he sobbed, "I never took your money, man!"

"You think I'm fuckin' stupid Bobby?" Jack asked. "I saw you with Lauren this morning, leaving my house. Now how do you explain that?"

Bobby spat out a tooth, "Jack, she's scared of you man. I was just trying to help. And I don't know shit about your money, I swear to God! Maybe Lauren—" *Crack!* Bobby saw stars as his head bounced off of the car hood again, this time leaving a dent. Blood swirled into the depression, gushing from where Bobby's front teeth had been.

"Lauren loves me, Bobby Boy. She'd never run to a scumbag like you." Jack cocked his fist for another blow and swung hard, but spun on his heels as his fist met air. Bobby had dodged, throwing him off balance. Jack hit the ground in a drunken stumble, which only enraged him further.

Seizing the opportunity, Bobby looked for something he could use to defend himself. He noticed a large wooden plank in a ditch next to the road, and dove for it, but Jack was faster. He tackled Bobby and easily wrenched the plank from his grasp. Standing over the cowering teen, Jack raised the plank over his head. Bobby knew Jack well enough to know he would show no pity.

Jack cackled into the night. He feinted at Bobby with the makeshift club a couple of times, as Bobby flinched and groveled. "Look at you. Pathetic." Jack spit at the ground, then hurled the plank into the dark field beyond. "I don't need that to deal with you," he grumbled through clenched teeth, grabbing Bobby by the collar. He drew back his fist to strike the knockout blow.

A shrieking, guttural howl erupted from the fields across the road. It was wolf-like, but different, twisted. Jack and Bobby looked at each other with eyebrows raised, then towards the source of the sound. Jack dropped Bobby to the ground as a greasy, hulking shape trotted out of the tall grass and toward them. As their eyes focused, they beheld a creature that resembled a huge, muscular dog, but it appeared to have been skinned alive. Wiry muscle tissue and bone glistened in the streetlight. It was oozing and bleeding, leaving a pool of black gore where it sat, patiently, staring at them. It was holding the discarded plank in its mouth.

With a rumbling growl, the thing dropped the plank onto the cracked asphalt of the old, desolate road. It stared at them with bulging, bloodshot eyes and panted heavily, its head cocked to one side. The beast barked a single, hopeful yip. With that it sprung to its feet and trotted back into the tall grass from whence it came.

"What the fuck was that?" Jack whispered.

"I... I dunno man. The friggin' thing had no skin!"

Their speculation was cut short with another loud yelp, followed by a blood-chilling wail that pierced the otherwise silent night.

The two stood there, dumbfounded. "Let's go, man," Bobby uttered, finally.

"'Let's'?" Jack replied, sarcastically. "Walk home, you piece of shit. I don't give rides to thieves." Jack burst out in smug laughter, then jingled the keys in his coat pocket. "Bye-bye, Bobby Boy! Have fun with your new pet!"

As if on cue, the ghoulish beast burst from the field once again. "Shit!" The two yelped in unison. The dog-thing loped over to them, dropped the plank at their feet, and took a few steps back. This time its posture was more aggressive, its head lowered, the glistening flesh on its face seemed contorted into a malevolent smile.

"Hey... you ugly fuck. You wanna fetch the stick? Huh? *Huh*?" Jack sang nervously, as he kneeled down slowly to retrieve it. "Good doggy, good dog..." Jack clenched the stick firmly, and in one deft move, lunged at the creature. The blow came down hard, but again, he missed entirely; the beast had easily dodged his attack. It retaliated with a precision lunge at Jack's throat and the sheer weight of the animal and its spastic thrashing nearly ripped his head clean off.

Everything had happened so fast, Bobby was still rising to his feet. "Jesus Christ!" The dog-thing turned to face Bobby, who promptly soiled himself. "G-g-good d-dog," he said as he stood there, frozen with fear. The thing wrenched the stick from Jack's dead, twitching hand and trotted over to Bobby. It dropped the stick at his feet, then sat down and waited, its tail flicking droplets of blood as it twitched from side to side. "W... Wanna play fetch?"

The beast replied with a single, optimistic yip. Bobby picked up the plank, slowly, and turned away from the beast. He cocked back and threw the stick with all he could muster, into the dark field beyond. The thing launched after it with incredible speed.

Bobby lurched into action once the ghastly beast was out of sight. He wrenched the car keys from Jack's coat pocket, nearly vomiting on top of Jack's grisly, beheaded corpse. Staggering, he fumbled into the car, cranked it into gear, and floored it. Adrenaline coursed through his veins as his mind tried to unravel what had just happened.

Glancing into the rearview mirror, Bobby screamed. He could see the dog galloping after him. It was keeping pace! Its sinewy jaws still clamped firmly to its wooden prize.

 After a few minutes (and at reckless speeds), Bobby regained his composure and slowed down, bringing the car to a stop under a dim highway streetlight. Something from within spoke to him, pleaded, though he couldn't really understand it. Bracing for the worst, he felt compelled to do... something.

With an exasperated sigh, he relented and opened the passenger door. Not even twenty seconds passed before he heard a familiar sloshing sound. Bobby's eyes welled up in fear, unsure of what the next few moments would bring. Though thoroughly terrified, he steeled himself and waited.

With a sickening thud, and the crackle of exposed bone, the skinless hulk leapt into the passenger seat of the car and dropped the plank onto Bobby's lap.

On the verge of passing out from fear, Bobby steadied himself. He owed this strange creature his life, and no matter the cost, he would attempt to show it some gratitude. Sweating profusely, Bobby slowly reached out to the ghoulish thing, then lightly patted its bulbous head. The dog-thing whimpered approvingly as he drew his hand back, now covered in a viscous red slime. Bobby wiped his hand on his jeans, then turned the key and started the car.

"Thanks, buddy," he finally said. "Well, uh... let's call you Ripper, I guess... You know, 'cause what you did to, uh, Jack and all." He chuckled nervously. Ripper thrust its huge maw forward and licked eagerly at Bobby's bruised face, lapping up blood from his missing teeth. Its withered, black tongue reeked of death, yet somehow, Bobby didn't mind. He smiled at the absurdity of it all. His most terrifying night ever, and it couldn't have gone better for him.

Now he had Lauren, Jack's money, and a loyal new pet.

Out in the Woods
(Continued from page 65 X1-3-1)

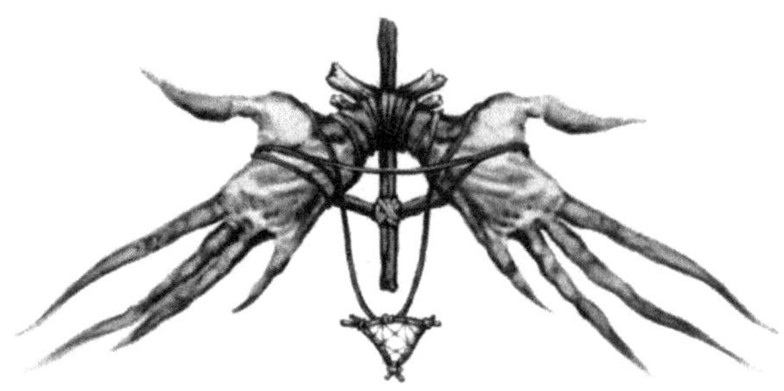

"We can come back for them with help," Mark said.

"Yeah," Jessie said. As heavy as it made her heart, she turned and ran through the trees.

The teens pumped their legs as hard as they could, their breaths heavy, now and then their sight filling with fog, only for it to fade. Then the trees opened up on the road.

"There's my car!" Mark said. The four of them got inside, and Jessie expected the car to be as useless as their phones, but it sprang to life when Mark turned the key. He backed up, turned around, and floored it toward town.

"The police station is down that street to the left," Steph said. Mark changed lanes and started slowing before a red light. Steph turned to the back seat. "Are you two okay?"

"We should've gone back," Andy said.

"I'm sorry," Jessie said. She took his hand. "We'll get them help."

"They'll be okay," Steph said. "We'll make sure of it."

"Can this light fucking change?" Mark said. A few moments went by.

"Forget the damn light," Andy said. "There's nobody around anyway."

Mark turned left, but stopped almost immediately. The bony woman stood in the middle of the street ahead, her legs rooted in the asphalt itself, torn through it like it was nothing.

"You guys see it too, right?" Mark asked.

A deep, calming voice entered Jessie's head, louder than any of her friends could talk.

Come to me, children.

"She's calling," Steph said.

"Ignore it!" Jessie replied, but even as she said it, she saw her hand reach for her door.

"Fuck that!" Mark shouted. He turned on the child locks, shut his eyes, and floored the gas.

Jessie grabbed on to Andy's hand and the back of Steph's seat. Steph grabbed one of the ceiling handles. The engine revved loudly, the hazy noise grew deafening and the fog was blinding, but then it was all gone. Mark slammed on the brakes, the tires screeched, and then the night was silent. In the distance behind them, the light finally turned green.

They were silent for a long time. "Is it gone?" Steph asked.

Jessie took her phone from her pocket. The time showed 1:49.

"For now," she said. She called Melissa, but the phone went straight to voicemail. Andy tried calling John, but the same thing happened.

Nobody believed any of the teens' story, and in the following weeks, they found no sign of Melissa or John. The only thing that kept the others out of jail was that there was also no sign of foul play.

They grew apart from each other over the years, and if they did talk, it was never about what happened in the woods. Jessie never owned a television; she couldn't handle hearing white noise, and she stayed inside on foggy days. She kept an analog watch on her at all times, and avoided looking at her phone whenever possible. She couldn't handle watching the minute digit stay the same.

Smile
by
David J. Lovato

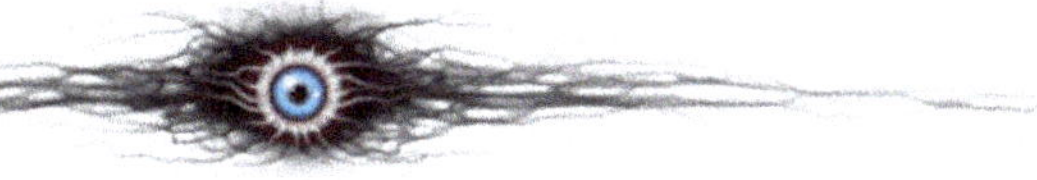

"Just smile," they say.
"Feeling down?
Inside-out?
Just smile!
All your problems go away!
Put a smile on your face!"
So I smile.
In the shower, where the water hides my tears, I smile.
Lying awake at night,
In a pitch black room where nobody can see
(especially not me)
I smile.
On the subway,
In a cubicle,
Near midday,
At a funeral.
As I write until the pencil wears down,
My fingertips wear down,
Graphite turns red but I have to get this down,
Or else I'll forget,
I smile.
As I walk until my shoes fall off,
My toes go numb and I lose skin in spots,
I run and run and run away,
But still end up in this same place,
I smile.
As I work my hands down to the bones
And then at night go home alone,
And wait to do it again first thing tomorrow,
I smile.
As I split open my chest,
Rip my heart from it,
Expose every demon who lives in my head,
I smile.

I smile so you won't forget.

Out in the Woods
(Continued from page 105 X2-1)

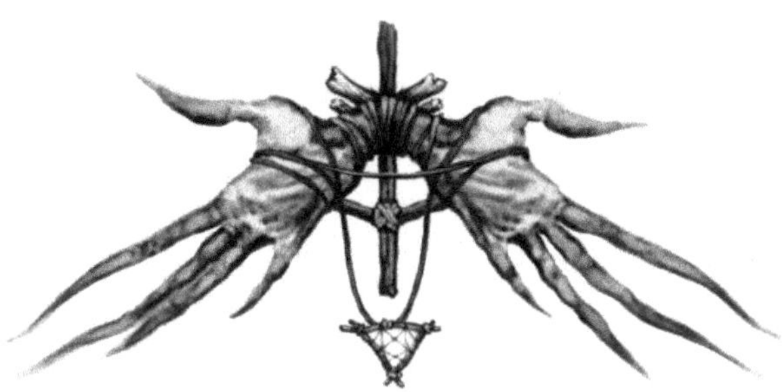

Jessie crawled to Andy's sleeping bag and gently shook him. "Hey, Andy."

Andy rolled over, saw Jessie hovering over him, and sat up. "Jessie? What's up?"

"My phone's not working, and it sounds like there's an animal or something nearby. I'm kind of scared."

Andy looked over Jessie's phone. He took out his own and realized it was doing the same thing. "Hey, guys!" he said. "Get up!"

Jessie hadn't expected him to wake everybody, but she almost immediately felt better as the others stirred.

"Andy, what the hell?" Melissa said.

"Check your phone. Is anyone's working?"

Any anger turned to confusion. "Mine's not," Steph said.

"Same here," Melissa replied.

"Guys," Mark said. "Do you see that?"

He was pointing out of the clearing. John rolled over, took the flashlight from his backpack, and tossed it to Mark. He turned it on and aimed it between the trees.

Out of the clearing, nestled between some of the trees, stood what looked like a skeletal woman. Her skin was pale and thick with ridges, matching the bark of the maples surrounding her.

"Is this a prank?" Melissa said. "It's not fucking funny."

Fog billowed in their direction, it almost seemed to come from the bony woman. The hazy sound grew louder, and the teens watched wide-eyed as the woman's skin writhed and transformed, coming up from the ground before her and receding into it behind her; she didn't walk, she grew along the ground.

"Oh my God!" Steph said. The bony woman drew closer, into their clearing.

"Go go go!" Mark screamed, and everyone made a dash for the trees.

Jessie was pretty sure they were going the way they'd originally come from. She was following close behind Mark, and she could hear Andy panting behind her. She turned to look and saw him and Steph, but not John and Melissa. Jessie stopped, and the others stopped soon after.

"We need to keep going," Mark said.

"Where's Melissa and John?"

The teens looked around, Mark pointed the flashlight from tree to tree and through the gaps between.

"Fuck," Andy said. "John's leg! He must've fallen behind."

"We have to go back for them," Steph said.

"We'd be heading toward that... that thing," Mark said.

"We could keep going and come back with help," Andy added.

To go keep going, turn to page X2-1-2 (71).
To go back for the others, turn to page X2-1-3 (189).

The Winter of 1816
by
David J. Lovato

September the 13th, 1816

The captain has asked me to keep a diary of events. He says the request comes from Jennings's office. ~~I don't~~ I've never kept a diary in my life, but I suppose it cannot be so difficult to write down the day's events, what little they may be.

It's cold already. It's been snowing all week, an early winter to follow an absent summer. ~~I'm in~~ They built a small log cabin near the bank of the Illinois, and here I am alone and will be alone for weeks.

A treaty has been signed, so the Natives shouldn't bother me. I don't trust them to hold to it, and I might have told the captain to hang me where I stood instead of send me into the woods alone, amongst the snow and the winds and the Natives. But ~~the Gove~~ Jennings seems to think this treaty will hold, and the captain says I'm safe out here.

I'm not even sure what I'm doing. Am I a foot in the door of this new land the Natives have given us? Or a test to see how much this treaty means to them?

I can feel them watching. I haven't seen anything, and although I hear noises in the woods constantly, it's nothing I can't explain as wild animals or trees breaking in the cold. (By God, it's cold.) But I feel them. It's as though a shadow stands behind me at all times. It's worst at night, as I sit with a fire to keep me warm or light my reading. Or my writing, as I'm doing now.

I've moved away from the window. Not much, the cabin isn't large enough for that. But I do feel a little better, even if I'm colder. I think I'll put another log on the fire and try to get some rest.

September the 15th, 1816

I ~~eam~~ cannot continue to write so far from the fireplace. My hands are too cold, they shake until they stop moving entirely. It takes an hour to write a paragraph. I'll risk the feeling of being watched if it means I can tie up this diary and get some rest.

I saw a Native today, very briefly. I think it was of the Ojibwe tribe. I didn't see much more than the headdress, long and spindly plumes stretching apart from each other. Then it was gone.

I haven't been killed. Maybe this treaty will stand after all. Perhaps I'm paranoid. The Treaty of Detroit worked, after all.

Still, that feeling of being watched... That's not all there is to it. I feel as though I'm not wanted. I'm sure I'm not; nobody wants me. The Natives want me off their land, the company wants me out of their hair out here, and the animals want me least of all.

They might have at least given me a dog to keep me company, or defend me from Natives or wolves. Maybe they'll bring one with the next supply run.

I've made a decision: If they bring me a dog, they want me alive. If they can't spare one, they must have little hope for this treaty, and less hope for my survival.

September the 17th, 1816

They didn't bring me a dog, but they said they will in four days' time. They want me alive, then. Just not very badly.

The crates of food and furs take up most of the cabin. I'm all right with this. It traps the heat in, and it blocks the window besides. Not all the way of course, but if anyone wanted to watch me, they'd have to do it from the trees.

September the 18th, 1816

I was out cutting trees to use for firewood. I had already done a small dead one, and then I moved on to a bigger one. I noticed something of a symbol carved into its bark. It didn't look like any of the Native symbols I'm accustomed to. It looked like a mixture of animals, a great deer or perhaps an elk, but its horns were spread wide, like the wings of a bird, if maybe it had only a few feathers left.

I ~~couldn't~~ don't know why, but I left the tree alone. It will surely be cut down if the others come to settle this land, but I won't touch it. As I stood staring at the carving, never before had I felt so followed, so watched. I took what little wood I had cut and went inside.

Maybe I'm being foolish. I'll have to cut more wood tomorrow, now. But it's not as though I have anything better to do.

I heard something just now. A branch falling, most likely. The wind has picked up. I pray I have enough wood to get through the night.

September the 21st, 1816

They brought the dog. I call him Walden. He seems to like me. He runs off for hours, and returns with small mammals. It's useful, but if I were attacked, he'd be miles away and of no help. He's not quite large enough to be of much help anyway.

A curious thing happened as I was talking with the supply man. A Native came out of the woods, hoping to trade with him. They did, and all went well. When they were done I asked the Native how many of his people are out here in the woods. He said he was the only one. I told him I'd seen an Ojibwe warrior in full headdress. He said that was impossible, the Ojibwe don't live this far out, and never have. I told him I must have been mistaken, the tribes all dress alike enough. He says if there are Natives in this area, he's never seen them.

So I'm alone out here, if I'm to believe this Native. (He gave me no reason not to.) I'm not sure if that makes me feel better, or worse.

The Native told me a curious story, as the Natives often do. He told me to watch myself, for a legend of his people tells that a man once grew so proud, he tried to claim he was the summer sun. That man was made to suffer a night so cold, he became the winter itself. After that, the Native went into the woods.

I had to pay with some of my rations, but I got the supply man to leave me a few traps. I'll be fine without the rations, the dog brings in enough food. I'll set the traps around the cabin, and hope ~~the dog~~ Walden doesn't step in them.

They say men go mad out here, alone. But I'm not so alone; there's a supply run every week, the only Native I've seen is friendly enough, and now I have the dog. Still, in the dark of night, as Walden sleeps and I'm left with only the wind and the crackling of the fire, I feel as though I'm the only man on earth, and the only other living thing is whatever's out there, watching me.

Enough of that. This diary will read like the ravings of a madman. There's no one out there watching me.

September the 24th, 1816

Every day is colder than the last, and every night colder than the day. Walden has taken to sleeping upon my bed, and we're both warmer for it.

I've seen no activity worth reporting, except a curious incident I took note of when I woke this morning. I stepped outside the cabin to relieve myself, and all of my traps had been set off, yet all were empty, and the snow was ~~untouche~~ absent of blood or tracks.

Branches and twigs fall from the trees almost as common as snowflakes, but some of the traps had nothing near them. Perhaps I was given faulty traps, and the wind was enough to set them off.

I reset the traps, and even watched for a while to see if any of them would go off. None did. I checked back later in the day and all remained set. I'll check again tomorrow.

September the 25th, 1816

All of the traps were buried under a fine layer of snow. None had gone off again. I had to spring them myself so I could dig them out and set them again.

Nothing of interest happened today. Still no sign of Natives, unless these strange goings on are their doing after all. Somehow I don't think that's the case. What kind of man can set off traps but leave no evidence? I myself had to use branches and set them off from clear away, yet when I found them yesterday some were undisturbed. I might say someone cleared away the rubbish, but for what? And anyway, there were no footprints, and it didn't snow yesterday nor the day before.

Regardless, I am still alive. Frozen to my bones, but alive.

Walden is barking in his sleep. I think he's cold, the noble beast. He's caught our dinner every night, I've yet to even open my latest case of rations. A man might live like this out here.

That is, if not for the never-ending feeling of being watched.

September the 28th, 1816

The supply man came a little later than usual, but he came. He says the snows slow him down.

I asked how long they want me to stay out here. He said he didn't know, he just delivers the supplies to me and men in the same position as me.

I half-hoped to see the Native from last time, but it was just me and the supply man. His name is Bartholomew Charles. It struck me as odd that I'd met him so many times, that my life depends on him, and I didn't learn his name until today.

My name is Ernest Lafayette. I hadn't written it in this journal yet; I'm not sure why I'm doing so now. In all likelihood, ~~they won't~~ no one will ever read this but me.

Unless, of course, something happens to me out here.

October the 1st, 1816

I didn't sleep last night. It was the coldest night I've seen out here, yet I was feverish, kicking the blankets from me only to freeze, and still I couldn't stop sweating. I must have come down with something.

All through the night I heard noises. It was like something was running around beneath the trees, hitting the lower branches so they almost made a tune.

Of course it was the wind. What else would it be?

It's early morning now, and I feel better, but not quite well. Still I must go out and cut more wood for the fire. I can barely stand as it is, but if I don't cut any wood, I'll freeze, and so will Walden.

October the 4th, 1816

I'm much better now. No more fever.

I heard the noises again last night, the ones I heard on the 1st. I'm beginning to think there's a deer running around my cabin at night. Maybe I'll catch it; I've had about enough of squirrel to last me a lifetime. Walden is a good dog, but he can't catch much else.

October the 6th, 1816

Bartholomew asked me to go through my journal and write up a separate letter including any happenings with the Natives. I can't help but feel that I was supposed to come home today, but they want me out here a little longer. I'm angry. I want to go back to civilization, and instead I'm here like a caged animal they can dangle in front of the lions to see how long it takes them to bite.

My letter included nothing. I won't tell them about the traps or the noises or the feeling of, because they're probably nothing. They can read about it when they get the whole diary if they wish, but I don't think they will. This book has become more personal, and if anybody reads these pages, it'll be me several years from now, sitting in a warm house by a warm fire somewhere in Indiana or maybe Massachusetts.

If I told them about the things I see and hear now, they might bring me back, but only to send me straight to the institution. Better to keep quiet now, and read these pages years from now and laugh at how silly I've been.

October the 8th, 1816

The traps were all set off again this morning, and again, there was no sign of what caused it. It did snow during the night, but not much.

That sound was louder than ever, or perhaps just closer. I wish it were a deer and would have been caught in one of the traps; Walden refused to go outside today. He growls if I try to push him through the door. I have ~~some~~ enough rations for a few days, but I've come to rely on him catching small game. I don't know ~~how long~~ that I'll make it if he stops.

October the 10th, 1816

I finally got Walden to go outside again. The dog acts as though nothing ever happened. Strange creature. Still, that was a close one, and I must hope he doesn't refuse to catch our dinner again.

October the 12th, 1816

I thought I saw something in the night. I had to go out to relieve myself, which I try to wait until morning to do, but every man has his moments of weakness. ~~Anyway, it~~

It was dark out, with only a solitary candle near the window to offer me any light. I made careful to avoid my traps and went as far as the tree line, and no farther.

It was cold, so I hurried. I turned to head back to the cabin, but bumped into a tree. I fell into the snow, and immediately got back up. I've heard tales of men who fall into the snow out here, and before long they start to feel comfortable, even warm. Those are the ones who never leave the snow, not unless someone comes to dig them out.

I used the tree as support when I stood up, and my hand traced over something odd. I couldn't see, but I felt around, and when I realized I was frightened, it occurred to me what it was: That carving I found, the one of the elk with an eagle for a head (if that's what it was).

I suddenly wanted very badly to be back inside the cabin. Try as I might, I couldn't see the candle I left lit by the window. I couldn't see much of anything; the clouds covered the moon, so my world was a shade of black with a lighter shade for the ground and a few darker ones marking the nearest trees.

I pushed back against the fear and waited for my eyes to adjust. I'd have to see the candle soon, or at least a dark spot interrupting the snow on the ground, indicating my cabin. Only seconds later, I heard that noise, the one of the lower ~~trees~~ branches being rattled. It was all around me, sometimes only metres away, and then I realized there was no wind. I felt nothing, the world was still, save for whatever was running through the darkness around me.

A deer, then, but I realized it couldn't be. I would hear it just beside me, and then somewhere far away, and then behind me, and then farther still, all in a matter of seconds. If it was an animal, it was more than one. Once, my eyes happened to be focused right where the sound was, and I saw what looked ~~light~~ like a shadow moving among shadows.

Against my better judgment, I called out for Walden. He barked in reply, and then I knew the cabin was to my left. I'd gotten more turned around than I thought.

As soon as I called out, the noises stopped. I might've been alone again. I made my way back to the cabin, and there the candle was, right where I left it, lit still. I don't know why I couldn't see it from outside.

That's when I realized just how odd things had been. I turned and bumped into that tree, but I'm certain I didn't walk past any when I first went out, and I know I didn't turn, so how could it have been behind me?

It was dark, and I was tired. I must have been confused. In any case, I am reminded just how dangerous it is out here. There may not be any Natives, but there is always the nature, and a man who doesn't respect its power is likely to get lost or frozen or killed by a wild beast.

October the 15th, 1816

Bartholomew hasn't come since the 6th. He's late, and I'm low on supplies. Walden goes out every day, but he hasn't come back with anything since yesterday.

I went out to cut wood today. I had an idea I should have ignored, but curiosity got the better of me. I decided to find that tree, the one with the carving.

With every step I took since deciding to find it, I felt more like I was being watched. Then it got worse; it was as though I were being followed. I kept looking over my shoulder, but I saw nothing and heard nothing. So why did it seem like something was behind me, and getting closer?

Walden barked in the distance, and that gave me courage. I wish it hadn't.

I found the tree with the carving. It's behind the cabin and six or seven trees in. There is no earthly way for it to have gotten behind me that night. I went straight out the cabin's only door, I didn't turn at all, in fear of getting lost or stepping in one of my traps.

And I did see the traps. There's one right by the tree with the carving. To think I might've stepped on it as I was lost out here. I hate writing that. I didn't get 'lost' because I know I went straight out.

Anyway, I moved that trap far away from the carved tree. I don't know why, but it seemed like a good idea.

October the 17th, 1816

Bartholomew came today. It's about time. I told him he was late and he insisted he wasn't any later than he's ever been. He's a good man, but he's a little confused, and my survival depends on him having a clear head. I can't very well tell him to come sooner next time if he keeps insisting he wasn't late, so I let it go. He's the only other human being I ever see, I'd much rather we get along.

October the 20th, 1816

I caught a deer in one of my traps. Good thing, too. I won't have to worry about food for a while. I've already skinned and cut the thing. I used an empty crate to store the excess meat, and I'll put it in the river to keep it cold.

I haven't heard those noises since.

I've said before and will say again that I've been foolish out here. I'm not alone, the woods are full of animals. I've caught one, so I know now ~~anyth~~ that anything out here is only as strange as I think it to be.

I wrote a letter recommending this spot for future development. They could build a whole village here. I made sure to recommend they cut down the trees behind this cabin. Maybe they can make it a nice little farm. They can do what they want; once I leave, I'm not coming back.

October the 24th, 1816

Bartholomew came, right on schedule. He gave me some supplies, and I bartered for more traps. (I still have enough of that deer to last a while.) I also gave him my letter. He said he'd be sure to deliver it to the company.

October the 25th, 1816

Walden didn't return this afternoon. I've no idea where he went. I hope he didn't get lost or injured out there.
I went out from the cabin as far as I dared, but I didn't hear nor see any sign of him. I hope he returns soon, it's getting dark out.
I waited up as long as I could. I've seen no sign of Walden. I have to shut the door and put out the candle.
It's so cold. I hope he's okay out there. Once or twice I thought I heard him returning, but there was nothing out there.

October the 26th, 1816

My crate in the river must have come loose. It's gone, along with the rest of the deer. I have nothing but my rations now, most of which I had traded for more traps. I'll have to eat lightly until Walden comes back. Or, it pains me to say, Bartholomew does.

October the 29th, 1816

It snowed for three straight days. When it was done I could barely open the cabin door.
The traps were all buried, and when I dug them out they were empty. I set them again. I need to catch something soon. My rations are nearly gone.

November the 1st, 1816

No sign of Bartholomew. The snow must be slowing him down.
I rarely sleep now. There's too much noise outside my cabin, that shaking and rattling again. It must be a deer, and I wish it would step in my traps already. I need to eat.

Anyway, it's too cold to sleep. Every morning I cut down a small tree, and it's gone by the next. My fire is always going, but I don't feel any warmer. When are they going to let me go home?

November the 3rd, 1816

My morning routine now includes setting all of the traps in addition to cutting down another tree. There's never anything in them, they're always just sprung but empty.

I wish Walden would come back. I need to eat.

November the 5th, 1816

I have to venture farther and farther to find a tree to cut for firewood. There's always the one, but I still won't touch it.

My rations are gone as of today. I stretched them as long as I could. I don't know what I'll do now. Bartholomew has to get here tomorrow or the day after, and then I'll be all right.

November the 6th, 1816

This will be the last time I write in this diary. Something must have happened to Bartholomew, but the company will realize it and send someone out. Not to get me, but to get my diary. It's all they wanted, after all.

This morning I went out early, with my axe. I'm so hungry I could barely lift it. I went past the trees, into the woods, to wait for an animal to come by. I had hoped for one of the deer that keep me up so late, teasing me.

I stood still for hours, but nothing happened. The woods didn't even make a sound. It got darker and it started to snow, so I headed back toward the cabin. I passed that tree, the one with the carving. I still hadn't gotten the day's firewood.

I couldn't cut the tree down. My arms were too tired.

I went on past it. Cold, tired, and starving, I grew foolish. I must have walked a half hour before I realized I had no idea where the cabin was. How could I have gotten lost? That tree was right behind it. I looked around, but recognized nothing. I looked for my own footprints, but the snow was untouched, even just behind me.

I turned around and started back the way I'd come, thinking I must have passed the cabin. After a while of walking, I heard that rattling, like frozen branches hitting against each other, or maybe dried bones.

I stood still. Maybe I'd catch dinner after all. There, to my left, the sound. I turned my head slowly, so slowly. Nothing there. The sound now ahead of me, I squinted and saw nothing. There the sound again, still to my left. Closer now. And again, just behind me. I turned, raising the axe.

I don't remember if I screamed. If I did, it did not echo against the trees. The world was silent as the grave as I fell backward, landing to sit in the snow.

Before me stood the creature from the carving. I'm sure of it. It was like an elk, larger than any I've ever seen or even heard a man tell of. Its horns were like the wings of a gigantic bird, stretching outward and upward to scrape the nearest trees and lowest branches. They were white as bone, long and winding, stretching into points so fine they might've been sharpened.

The creature had no skin. It was all bone, all yellow and white. I could see through its ribcage, into the forest beyond. Only its heart remained in its chest, more black than red. The beast must have frozen and been picked at by wild animals years ago.

Then the heart beat, and the beast lowered its head to look at me.

It had no eyes. They'd have rotted long ago, probably first. Still it stared at me, from pits blacker than any night I've suffered out here. In my heart I knew as true as God made men that it was looking at me. It snorted without breath, a large, percussive sound, yet no smoke came forth, and nothing moved.

It raised its great, wide head, its horns clattering against the frozen branches, sprinkling snow and ice down, breaking off some of the smaller twigs. It raised a hoof and dropped it, silently. I knew then, this creature held all the power I thought I ever could.

It tilted its head, one side scraping higher into the trees, the other low, almost enough to touch the ground, surely low enough to pierce me, should it only step forward. As it moved it creaked and groaned like an old boat or loosened staircase.

The creature snorted again, and then it leveled its head and stepped forward. I closed my eyes; I couldn't bear to watch it run me through. Another step, then another, only to my right. I opened my eyes in time to see its powerful thigh bones twisting back and forth as the creature walked past me. When it was out of sight I listened for the creaking of bones, but heard nothing but the wind.

I don't know how long I sat there in the snow, but finally I gathered the courage to look behind me. I saw only the woods. The snow was red with the setting sun, and the trees cast shadows longer and darker than winter.

I stood up, left the axe where it lay, and somehow found the strength to run. My joints ached, my lungs and nose burned as I breathed the cold, but I ran.

I had to twist and turn to avoid the trees, each time taking more strength than the last. The world was getting darker; I wasn't sure if my eyes were closing or the night was coming on faster than I could run. Just when I thought I didn't have the strength to avoid another tree, a sharp pain clamped around my leg. I cried out, certain the creature had been just behind me the whole time, had stabbed one of its horns straight through me. I fell, turning as I did so, and saw only the dark forest behind me.

I looked at my leg and my heart sang to find I had stepped in one of my own traps. The cabin couldn't be far. I pried myself from the trap and stood. My leg was bleeding, but thankfully, the trap was one of the smaller ones. I turned, much slower, slightly limping, but glad to be near the cabin. I saw it soon after; I was behind it. All of my weariness caught up to me at once, and I fell against a tree to catch my breath.

I knew which tree it was, but I had to get my air. Once I did, I straightened and looked at the tree. It was the closest one to the cabin, the last one I hadn't cut down, but there was no carving. Its bark was full and untouched.

I went inside the cabin. Instantly I wondered why I had been so happy to find it; there's still no food and less warmth. It keeps most of the wind away, and does little else.

I retrieved my skinning knife and went back out to the tree. With the last of the day's light, I carved the creature into it, in the place I saw the carving before. My own carving bears a striking resemblance to the one I'd feared so long, if I say so myself.

I came back in to write this all down. When the company finds the cabin empty except for this diary, they will say I went mad out here, and in my madness wandered into the woods to freeze to death. They will try to find my body, but not very hard. I don't blame them. I have a feeling they could search forever and never find it.

I'm going into the woods now. I'm not mad; on the contrary, I see with a clarity few men are ever privy to. I see now that I tried to be greater than something greater than all mankind, and this is the price to be paid.

I have drafted a letter recommending the company not develop this land. Men aren't meant to live here, that's why there aren't any Natives. Perhaps I should have lied and said there were; maybe then the company would listen and leave this place alone. Somehow, I think not.

I've done what I can. I go now to an end few men can claim, and although I do not know what awaits me, I fear more for the next man the company sends than for myself, for I will know peace.

Ernest Lafayette
The Winter of 1816

Playtime
by
David J. Lovato

"Scissors!" Jane said, firmly but calmly. She couldn't get frazzled now; Teddy's life depended on her.

"Scissors," she said in a lower, more monotone voice: her assistant. Jane wiped sweat from her brow, then hooked one arm of the scissors into the small incision she'd made in Teddy's fur-like cloth. Carefully, methodically, she cut a ring around the top of his head, a few inches above his ears. A little bit of stuffing popped out with every snip.

"Here goes nothing," Jane said. She lifted the loose fur up and set it aside, leaving Teddy's cotton brain completely exposed.

Someone knocked softly at the door, and a second later, Jane's mother entered the room.

"Mom! You're interrupting Teddy's surgery! The room has to stay sterile!"

Jane's mother closed the door, then spoke from the other side. "Sorry, Janey! But it's past your bedtime. Another surgery? Already?"

"This one's important!" Jane said. "This one will make Teddy alive for real!"

Jane's mother laughed. "Is that so?"

"It's a total brain transplant! He had a bad case of cottonbrain."

"Well, Dr. Jane, I don't want to rush Teddy's surgery, but it's time for bed. Try to finish up soon?"

"Almost done," Jane said. Footsteps pattered down the hall, and Jane set back to work, removing all of the fluff from Teddy's head. When she was finished, she took the new fluff, the stuff she'd found in a dusty old box in the attic marked with *Don't Touch!!!*, and filled his head to the brim.

Jane realigned Teddy's scalp, took her thread and needle, and began stitching him back together. The worst was over, but stitching back together was far from easy. It seemed to take forever, and now both Teddy's life and her mother's wrath were on the line.

Finally, Jane snipped the thread away, and Teddy was finished. She held him up to inspect him: Stitches criss-crossed his skin all over, some of them coming loose after months of play, one of his eyes threatening to fall out.

"That'll have to be your next surgery," Jane said. She hugged Teddy close. "Someday you'll be a real bear, just like I'll be a real doctor."

Jane yawned wide, then looked at her supplies lying around. She should clean up, but it was already late. She'd leave it for the morning. Jane took Teddy in her arms, turned the nightlight on, flicked off the overhead light, and climbed into bed.

Teddy stood up. It was hard; he'd never quite done it on his own before. He looked at his friend, Jane, glowing softly in the orange-red of the night light. He pressed a soft paw against her face, but she didn't move. What was wrong with her? She'd been fine only minutes before. Playtime was only beginning, and Teddy could finally move on his own, finally think and feel, so why was Jane not responding?

Teddy looked around. He remembered everything, thought back to the countless times she'd fixed him. Jane was always so kind to him; now it was Teddy's turn to repay the favor.

Teddy hopped off the bed, hobbled over to the supplies on the ground, and gathered the scalpel and scissors. Carefully, step by stumpy step, he waddled back to Jane's bed, emptied his armful onto it, then climbed up. He took the scalpel in his paw, walked across Jane's chest, and rested above her. Where was it she'd fixed him? Oh yes, the head. Teddy pressed he scalpel against Jane's skin.

Don't worry, Jane. I'll patch you up, and then playtime will begin.

Out in the Woods
(Continued from page 65 X1-3-2)

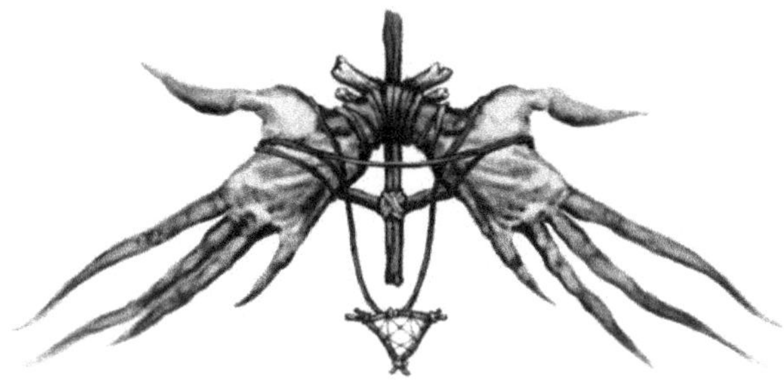

"We have to go back," Jessie said. She started back the way they'd come.

"Wait," Andy said. He found a sharp rock and carved an arrow in a nearby tree. "In case we get turned around."

The four teens headed among the trees.

"Melissa!" Steph shouted. "John!"

"Turn off the light," Mark said. "They have a flashlight too, maybe we'll see it."

Jessie turned off her light. Already she could hear faint white noise, and she thought she could see fog before her eyes.

"There!" Andy said. In the distance, a flashlight beam bounced among the trees, cut off here and there by tall stalks of darkness.

"Hey!" Jessie shouted. They started toward the light. "Melissa!"

"Jessie!" Melissa hugged her. "I don't know what happened, you guys were suddenly not there anymore."

"We're almost out," Mark said. "This way!"

He turned toward their marked tree, and froze. Both flashlight beams fixed on the same area, at the edge of which stood the tall woman, completely still, her pale hands lifted.

"What do we do?" John said.

"She's calling," Andy said. The others looked at him. He took a step toward the creature.

"Andy," Jessie said. Andy stopped. He almost turned his head toward her, but it was like he couldn't look away. He started another step, and Jessie took his hand.

Haze filled their minds, the fog worsened, and the creature was several feet closer. A thunderous but calm, not unpleasant voice filled Jessie's ears.

Come to me, children.

"She's calling us," Melissa said.

"Ignore it!" Jessie shouted.

Children, please.

Slowly the creature came closer, but only by a few inches.

"We can push it back!" Jessie said. She took Melissa's hand in one of hers, put the flashlight in her armpit, and took Andy's hand in the other. The six teens all held hands.

Come to me, where you belong.

"Go away!" Jessie screamed.

The static sound got quieter, the fog thinned almost to invisibility. At the edge of the light, faint in its glow, the creature stood tall, unmoving. Quietly, she laughed.

But you belong with me.

The fog and sound vanished, and she was gone.

The group stood for a moment, waiting to hear that sound or see the fog, or anything moving out in the woods. Nothing did. Jessie had an idea; she let go of Melissa's hand and carefully took out her phone, trying her hardest not to move the flashlight. A wide smile appeared on her face when she saw the time: 1:45

"It's gone," she said.

It didn't take long to find their arrow tree, and shortly beyond it, the trees broke and gave way to the road. Mark checked his GPS.

"We parked down that way."

Together, the group started toward their cars. Steph gave Mark a big hug, and Jessie smiled and took Andy's hand.

She knew ahead lay sleepless nights, restlessness, that she would never hear wind or rain or look at fog the same way, and that in a sense, their troubles were just beginning. But they had each other, they would always have each other, and at least for now, they were out of the woods.

Thirteen Stairs
by
David J. Lovato

Thirteen stairs downward descend,
But for each one a life must end.
And at the bottom lies a prize,
Befitting whomever survives.

Smith found the stairs, that part was easy
But the rest was none too pleasing.
So Smith went to the town fool,
And pushed him down tied to a stool.

How he cried and how he wept,
Until on the stairs he slept.
Next Smith found the baker's son,
And pushed him down another one.

Eleven steps now left to go,
Smith found a stray cat in the road.
And sure it yelped, and yes it whined,
But on the stairs it lost its life.

Standing now near the tenth step,
Smith began to feel regret.
But he could almost taste his prize,
So down went old man Valentine.

Those wretched twins, Bobby and Kate
Made fodder for steps nine and eight.
Seven was a hitchhiker,
And six a bar hopping biker.

With all those disappearances,
The town was full of fearfulness.
But that would not stop Smith, you see,
So next up was the police chief.

People locked their doors at night,
And kids would not go play outside.
But the prize was calling louder,
Smith would soon now have its power.

A drunkard stumbling toward his home
Took a turn down the wrong road
He ended up down on stair four,
And three went to the man next door.

Smith took a while to find step two,
Taking a shortcut to school.
The little brat did not get far
When Smith ran over him with his car.

Just one to go now, one last step
But there was no one left to get.
So Smith went home to his own wife,
And let the last stair take her life.

Thirteen steps now, not one more
And at the bottom was a door
But when Smith finally opened it,
He found only a janitor's closet.

This wasn't right, this couldn't be!
It wasn't fair, he'd won, you see!
So Smith took his own life right there,
At the bottom some might call a stair.

Fourteen bodies, fourteen stairs
Unlocked the hidden portal there
Out crept a doom for all mankind,
Who'd kill thirteen just for a prize.

Out in the Woods
(Continued from page 166 X2-1-3)

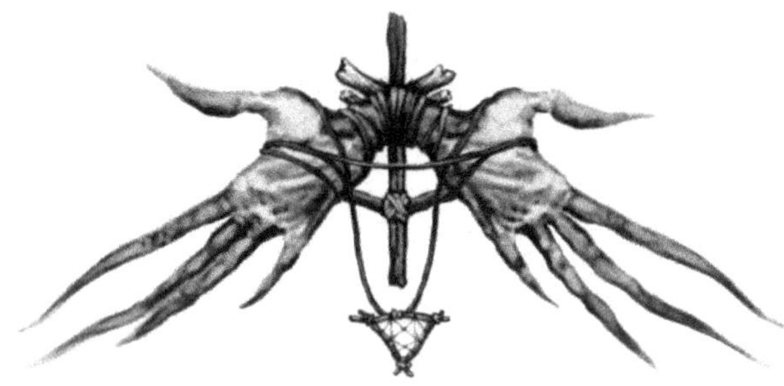

"We have to go back for them," Jessie said.

"Yeah," Andy replied. The four teens turned and headed back into the woods.

"Melissa! John!" Mark called. He frantically pointed the flashlight around, casting thin shadows along the ground. Every tree that was slightly more pale than brown put Jessie on edge; the creature could be anywhere.

"John!" Andy shouted. "Melissa!"

In the distance someone screamed, and then the woods were silent.

"It came from over there," Steph said. "I think."

"Yeah," Jessie said. The four of them moved in and out among the trunks of maples, the fog growing thicker around them, until they came to a tiny clearing. The ground squished under Jessie's foot. Mark shined his light that way, and Jessie lifted her shoe. The dirt below was bright red, and it was splattered up her shoe. Mark looked around the clearing, and the grass and trees were covered in red peppered with pink and white bits. Entrails hung from the branches above.

"Oh my God," Mark said. Steph threw up.

A calm, booming voice broke in, seemingly coming from all around:

Children. Come to me. Come to Mother.

At the edge of the flashlight's glow, the creature appeared. Her arms were outstretched for an embrace.

"Leave us alone!" Jessie screamed.

The static sound grew louder, the bony woman drew nearer.

"She's... calling me," Mark said. He took a few steps toward her, walking through the puddle of his friends' remains.

"Mark!" Steph screamed. "What are you doing?"

"Steph," Jessie said. Even as she protested, Steph was walking toward the creature, too.

The bony woman sprouted long, viny tentacles from her back. They wiggled in the air, silent.

Jessie took Steph's hand, and Steph stopped walking. Mark was almost out of reach, but Steph lurched forward and grabbed his. The four teens linked hands and stood their ground, the gaunt woman came ever closer, bringing thick billows of fog with her.

"You stay away!" Andy shouted.

Children, come with me. Come home.

"Fuck you!" Jessie screamed. The bony woman drew closer, but more slowly. She came to a near stop, still ten feet away. Jessie shut her eyes tightly, squeezed her friends' hands. "Leave!"

Just like that, the fog and the static were gone. The four teens stood in the woods, a gentle breeze blew.

Jessie let go of her friends and pulled out her phone: 1:46. She unlocked it with ease, and even the ground below them was dry, void of any sign of what had happened there.

The GPS led them out of the woods, back to the road, where their cars waited. As they walked, Jessie took Andy's hand again. He smiled, and she smiled back. She knew ahead would be sleepless nights, that nobody would believe their story, that they might even be blamed for what happened to Melissa and John. She pushed these thoughts from her mind; for right now, she and her friends were out of the woods, and they were going home.

*Qc zowbi tmiqyv-yeaw, aqcz
qci qwiqyvi etc. Qc seedi xet
qw czv vxvi, owy ipqsvi aqcz
qci petcz.*

The Vicar's Barn
by
Josh Leichliter

Marceline hated staying after school on Thursdays to attend her student career program, but her mother had insisted she enroll in the class anyway. It was worse on days like this; it was nearly 6 p.m., the sky was darkening as blocky grey clouds choked off the already scarce sunlight, and Marceline would have to walk home. Class ended, she grabbed her backpack from her locker, and trudged off on her hour long walk home. If she hurried, she might make it before dark.

Huge fields and pastures devoured the landscape in an industrious bid for dominance. Often Marceline would take a shortcut through a certain field, which hastened her travel considerably. This route was not without obstacles however, as it led her past a derelict farmstead. She'd have to climb through a few old barbed wire fences in her trespass, but they were rusted and slack with age.

Abandoned by time and partially destroyed by some historical fire, the house was little more than a skeleton of blackened timber. Thick brambles of weeds and twisted trees had reclaimed most of the foundation, snaking around charred support beams and husked walls. The looming barn, however, remained mostly intact, though it swayed as if it might blow over with the slightest gale.

Rumors told that this property was abandoned in the 60's by a defrocked priest, though nobody seemed to remember his crimes. The old man disappeared mysteriously after his house burned down. No remains were found, so it was generally assumed that he fled quietly after the fire. Over the years the property had gained a reputation for being haunted, as decaying places tend to do.

Being a proper skeptic, Marceline believed none of this, dismissing the rumors as small town gossip and superstition. Every landmark here had some outlandish tale attached to it; the people of Bethel County had a certain flair for the dramatic. The old farmstead did strike a sinister visage however, and it was no surprise that this place had some tragic tale in its repertoire.

***

The darkening clouds bore down with malice, and before long bursts of freezing rain assailed Marceline like a million tiny bullets. The torrent was relentless, the massive raindrops exploding on her skin with painful impact. She was drenched to the bone, frozen to the core, and completely miserable. She needed shelter, and the old barn was the only place for a mile. She'd always been a little spooked by the place, but she was certain it was far better in there than being assaulted by the machine-gun rain. As long as the barn didn't blow over with her in it... she hesitated.

Self-preservation persevered with a fresh crack of lightning and roar of thunder. Marceline ran fervently to the barn and wrenched at the old wooden door. Cemented with age, the door begrudgingly creaked open, just enough for her to squeeze through and out of the rain. She stood still in the door frame for a few moments, until her eyes adjusted to the dark. The inside of the barn was ribboned with sinister-looking shadows. A few angular streaks of light stabbed at the dark from cracks in the walls and ceiling. Rusted, antique tools clung to the walls and dotted various benches, while dust particles drifted aimlessly throughout the stale air. And there was a stench... putrid, oily and rotten.

Feigning confidence, Marceline found a musty old bale of hay and sat down. She stared into the darkness as her mind wandered. She tried to picture the daily activities that used to occur in this place, but her thoughts kept slipping away to more malignant realms. This place bothered her, though she couldn't make any logical sense of it. Slowly, the hair on her arms stood on end, as a nervous tingle slithered down her spine.

Marceline was beginning to regret her decision to seek refuge here. She generally gave the old barn a wide berth, for no other reason than she feared it might topple down on her. She occasionally teased herself with thoughts of vengeful ghosts and murderous madmen lurking within this place, but dismissed the silly notions just as quickly. Yet here she was, in the barn of imagined horrors. But this time her imagination was decidedly less whimsical.

The wind and rain outside smashed at the structure with all of mother nature's wrath. The creaking timbers and pelting rain played a clamorous melody, like some disparate steampunk symphony. The blaring noise worked to further demoralize her. Nervous, she spoke aloud to herself. "At least it's dry. Besides..." She laughed at the notion. "There's no ghosts, Marcy, get a grip."

It didn't take long until she noticed that the acrid odor of the barn began to grow stronger. It smelled like excrement and sulfur, and it made her gag. She choked back the urge to vomit and covered her mouth and nose with her sleeve. Apprehensive, she fumbled for her phone.

"Ugh, where is it?" she snapped aloud, frustrated. "Ah," she uttered when she found it. "I gotta organize my crap..." She trailed off as the world around her grew strangely oppressive and unnaturally still.

The rain on the roof, the crack of thunder, and the howling wind were gone. Everything became suddenly, sickeningly silent. She held her breath and waited, her own galloping heartbeat now drumming in her ears. A quick shuffle, somewhere in the murk... She swore she'd heard it. Just an animal she thought, running from the rain too. She exhaled a hesitant sigh of relief.

A deafening crackle erupted from one of the stalls near the back. Some massive thing thrashed violently in the rear of the barn! Marceline screamed aloud, the abrupt burst of noise shocked her so thoroughly that she fell backwards over the hay bale she was sitting on and smashed heavily into the ground.

Whatever was in that stall barreled toward her now, thrashing more violently, deafening as it neared. Her senses exploded, everything she knew as reality became fractured and distorted. The walls ruptured and heaved, the air pulsed with electricity and chaff, and her ears cracked with the thunderous racket.

Marceline scrambled to find footing. Her convulsive thrashing had left her entangled in a heap of old baling twine that was strewn across the floor. She became wrapped up in the cordage, and was now thoroughly panicked. She opened her mouth to scream, but only managed a sort of devastated, confused gurgle. She lay there ensnared, eyes wide and mouth agape, her jaws clacking in helpless terror.

Those few seconds may as well have been hours as she lay petrified with fright. That was when the most surreal manifestation occurred. A rasped, unearthly voice panted wetly in her ear. She could feel its stinking breath sear her skin. It was barely a whimper, but the words echoed painfully: "Buurned usss… I'm buuurning!"

Marceline turned toward the sound and found herself face-to-face with some ethereal monstrosity. It glared at her with icy blue cataract eyes, its flesh melted around bone, its singed hair plastered in bloody, wet clumps to its bulbous head. The thing's lips were burned away, exposing long, jagged teeth that snapped ferociously, mere inches from her face.

At this shocking culmination, Marceline managed the scream she had been choking back. Like a banshee, her shrill howl echoed throughout the barn, and beyond. To her horror, the occult sounds that erupted from within her were not hers. Demonic howls of a dozen wretched souls burst from her lips, piercing her own ears as she spat them forth. It was as though a thousand red ants were crawling in her throat, biting and stinging and suffocating her. Mortified, confused, and in severe pain, Marceline rolled onto her side and vomited.

Her sickness soon diminished and she kicked in reflex. Reality came back into focus. Her instinct to survive prevailed as she lurched into action, clawing at the wiry twine that held her and ripping it away from her limbs. Dashing towards the thin streak of light from the barn door, her salvation seemed a thousand miles away. She felt like she was running under water. The ghoulish thing was right on her heels, she could feel its acid breath licking at her neck as it shrieked tortured hymns into her ears.

"He buuurned usss," it wailed in desperate, tormented tones.

Marceline erupted from the barn, gashing her arm deeply on some rusted metal protrusion. Bleeding profusely, she never even looked back. Marceline ran for all her life. Her lungs heaved with pain when she finally reached her house; by then her arm had gone completely numb. She ran upstairs to her room, collapsed onto her bed, and sobbed. Pink sheets reddened as she lay there, bleeding in the solace of her perfect pink room, in her perfect white house.

She drifted in and out of consciousness as her father burst into her room, shouting something she couldn't hear. Her vision was blurry and colorless, her ears rang like ruined bells. The blood loss had taken its toll.

There was some commotion as the paramedics scurried to help the girl who was lying on her bed. Confused and shocked, the weight of this revelation soon became clear. Marceline observed the calamitous scene as one would a movie, as it drifted further and grew darker every second, until heavy black curtains came crashing down. She stared unseeing into the pitch black that now surrounded her, when she felt the icy, stinking breath of a familiar foe.

"Burn with me," it whispered.

197

The Piano
by
Sarah Carswell

Tobin stared at the old piano. He wasn't sure what to say.

"It needs to be tuned," his grandfather was saying, "and cleaned and polished. But it's a rare find, Tobin. It dates back to the eighteenth century. Beethoven himself may have played these very keys."

The old man waited for Tobin to reply, but the silence stretched on.

His grandfather sighed. "Look, Tobin," he said, "Cynthia—I mean your mother—once told me that you enjoyed playing piano. Maybe it would be good for you to get back to doing something that you enjoyed before... before..."

"Before your son murdered my mother?" Tobin asked calmly.

The old man's eyes flashed with anger. He lifted a hand to strike his grandson, but stopped himself in time. "You aren't the only one who has experienced pain, young man. You would be wise to remember that."

Left alone with his thoughts and the ancient piano, Tobin slumped on the old padded bench. Centuries' worth of dust wafted from the tapestried seat, irritating his asthma and causing him to wheeze. Why did he try to start fights with his grandfather? The poor old man was as much a victim as he was. He wanted no more to raise a teenager than Tobin wanted to be raised by an elderly hermit.

No, the only person who deserved his anger was his father, who drank too much and got unreasonable. His despicable, never-should-have-been-born father, who got drunk one night two months ago, convinced himself that his wife was having an affair, and killed her. Oh, it was an accident. He only meant to rough her up a little. But he went too far, just like he always did. And then what did that sorry excuse for a human do when he realized what he'd done? Did he face the consequences like a man? Of course not. He washed down his wife's bottle of sleeping pills with a bottle of whiskey.

In the end, he'd left his son and his father to pay for his own mistakes.

Bringing his breathing under control, Tobin ran his fingers along the ivory keys. His grandfather was right. The piano was a masterpiece. And he had enjoyed playing before... before. Tobin had wanted to take lessons, but advancing his son's musical ability hadn't gone along with his father's plans to spend every last dime he made on booze. In the end, Tobin had to be content with the occasional playtime and lessons that he could squeeze out of the old spinster who had lived in the apartment above theirs. He hadn't played particularly well, but it was one of few things in his life that he had enjoyed.

Tobin played a C chord, one of the only chords he knew. Despite its age and obvious lack of upkeep, the instrument sounded rich and resonant and surprisingly on-key. Tobin's fingers transitioned effortlessly to a G chord, one he hadn't realized he knew, and then they took off with a life of their own, spanning the keys and churning out an intense contrast of harmonies and melodies.

Gasping, Tobin ripped his fingers from the keys. He held his hands in front of his face, turning them over and staring at them as though he had never seen them before. How had he coerced such beautiful, haunting sound from this piano?

Breathing heavily, Tobin pressed a forefinger to one of the keys. As if of their own intellect, the rest of his fingers joined the one, traversing the ivories and milking them of their music, coaxing them of their evocative secrets from centuries past.

Tobin closed his eyes and leaned his head back, allowing the music to overtake him. Never had he felt so in control of himself, his surroundings. Never had he been worthy of something so memorable, so powerful.

As he played the starring role in his own private concerto, Tobin didn't feel his fingers melding with the ivory keys, nor did he sense the brass of the pedals fusing with his feet. He felt nothing besides the sheer force of the music that moved him to his core and refused to let him go. The more vigorously he played, the deeper he was drawn into the composition.

Choking, Tobin realized he couldn't breathe. Frantically, he gasped for air, but it was as though a vice had closed around his neck. He rolled his eyes downward to see ivory seeping upward through his fingers, spreading through his veins, up to his chest and neck.

Breaking out of the music's reverie, Tobin recoiled backward, attempting to break the physical connection that was growing by the second between the piano and himself. In a strangled voice he cried out for help, but the tempo increased, and his feet pressed harder on the pedals, amplifying the volume.

Determined to save his life in a way that he couldn't save his mother's, Tobin struggled to sever himself from the piano. He tore his left hand away from the keyboard, the ivory dripping from his fingertips like boiling taffy. Falling off the bench, he separated the connection with his right hand.

Able to breathe again, Tobin scrambled backward on the hard floor, desperate to disconnect his feet from the pedals.

"Grandfather!" he cried. "Help!"

Tobin examined the bond between his feet and the pedals. It was no use – they were literally welded together.

"Grandfather!" he cried again.

Tobin didn't see the piano strings, summoned by his struggle like a predator to its prey, creep from the instrument's mahogany case, down its legs, and along the floor to where he lay helpless. He didn't sense them going for the kill until it was too late, and even if he had, there wouldn't have been anything he could do to stop them.

The strings wrapped themselves around poor Tobin, like a snake around an immobile rat, and dragged him into the belly of their beast. The lid closed with a loud *thunk*.

The old man waited outside the door until all had been quiet for some time. Then, with a heavy sigh, he entered the room, sat down at the bench, and played a song filled with misery and rage.

Notes

Notes

Afterword

Crypto Bizarro, as a concept, was born five years ago, with a smattering of experimental watercolor paintings. I had never used the medium before; it was strange and unfamiliar, and I loved it. After some interesting results, ideas began to form and have evolved into what you see before you now.

The book was originally modeled to be a "spiritual successor" to the *Scary Stories to Tell in the Dark* series, a favorite from my youth. In keeping with that vision, the illustrations and writing were initially meant to be unsettling, even frightening, though palatable for younger audiences. We specifically avoided using profanity, nudity, drug use and overt gore, in an effort to keep it somewhat "clean." However, as years passed, the volume began to find its own voice, and evolved into something a bit murkier, stranger, and more mature. We began to include cryptograms, obscure puzzles, and more, in an effort to create a darker, more interactive experience.

As with the writing, the illustrations saw many iterations, tonal changes, and endless tweaks, before I settled on an art style that I felt would complement the phenomenal writing of the book. Artist Stephen Gammell was a huge influence in this, as well as other prolific talents such as Zdzisław Beksiński, H.R. Giger, Frank Frazetta, and Gerald Brom. Certainly all of these fantastic artists helped inspire my own work on Crypto Bizarro.

Nearly two-and-a-half years ago, in a stroke of blind luck, I met David, an experienced author who has since graciously lent his considerable talents to this project, and has created an air of legitimacy to what would otherwise have just been a stack of odd notes and scribbles. His writing, editing, and formatting skills are formidable, indispensable, and have helped shape this heap of odds and ends into something presentable. None of this would be possible without his enduring dedication and personal investment in this project.

The roller coaster was clinking its way up to the proverbial precipice. The inevitable drop was just ahead, and the brakes nonexistent. So… we invited some friends along for the ride! Sarah, Seth, Nick, Andrea, and Aerys hopped on board to endure this wild journey with us. Their contributions helped immensely in keeping this stalwart vessel on track, all the while allowing us a gander into their own personal Hellscapes.

We are so excited to share this endeavor with you, dear reader. Without you, Crypto Bizarro is merely a passing dream… or perhaps, a nightmare.

Josh Leichliter
November 2018

Josh and I met on Reddit in July of 2016. He had posted some of his art to overwhelmingly positive response, and quite a few people saw the influence of Stephen Gammell's illustrations for *Scary Stories to Tell in the Dark*. Josh had replied that he would love to collaborate on a collection of short stories, and wanted to reach out to other writers.

I immediately fell in love with the illustrations he had posted, and didn't hesitate to offer to help in any way I could. I've seen a lot of artists try to emulate Gammell's style over the years, and Josh is the only one who let inspiration stay inspiration, and let his own style shine through.

Over the following two years, we traveled a long and winding path through the dark forests of our minds, reached out to some of our writer friends, kept in touch, and slowly but surely made progress on the collection you now hold in your hands.

We threw everything at the wall for this one. We wanted to make something odd, off-the-wall, crazy, scary, mysterious, and fun, both for us in creating it, and for those reading it.

I'm so happy with the way it turned out, and with the experience as a whole. I look forward to working with Josh and the rest of this team in the future. None of this would be possible without Josh, Sarah, Seth, Andrea, Aerys, and Nick, and you have our deepest gratitude for indulging in our dark fantasies with us.

David J. Lovato
November 2018

About the Authors

David J. Lovato is a creator and destroyer of worlds whose other works include several novels, short story collections, poetry collections, and a zombie apocalypse series co-authored with Seth Thomas. You can find more info at www.davidjlovato.com.

Josh Leichliter whiles away his days on strange, creative pursuits. Eighteen years in the video game industry have allowed him to try his hand at multiple disciplines, including writing, level design, animation, sound design, sculpture, 3D modeling, illustration, and art direction. A freelancer ever searching for his next adventure, you can contact him at sycheos@ymail.com

Sarah Carswell has been writing for as long as she or anyone else can remember. She lives in Arizona with her husband, two children, three dogs, a cat, and a tortoise. When Sarah isn't spinning twisted stories and poetry from the darkest corners of her mind, she shapes the bright minds of the future in her fifth grade classroom. Follow her on Instagram @_the_tattooed_teacher.

Seth Thomas is a writer and lover of all things horror. His other works include a novel and several short stories, as well as a zombie apocalypse series co-authored with David J. Lovato. You can find more info at his website, sevidian.wordpress.com.

Nicholaus Brown is a freelance writer and has been an accomplished video game artist for thirteen years. He lives in Texas with his four boys, the woman who put a spell on him, and three rescued dogs that poop too much. Contact him before the apocalypse on Twitter @goatGHOST.

Aerys Bates-Leichliter is a lanky raccoon who enjoys drawing trash and memeing out 'til 3 a.m. You can find her at lankyslothlady@yahoo.com

Andrea Wright enjoys writing, and is an accomplished artist, muralist, and lover of all things equine. She can be found at gingerbreadearth@gmail.com

*Wlwmi zhhj et x
shhmfxi zwkfwwc
fhmnst. Fbxk ses ihq
qcnwxtb fbwc ihq
hawcws kbet hcw?*